BICKERING BIRDS

A COZY CORGI MYSTERY

MILDRED ABBOTT

D1523387

WINGS OF INK PUBLICATIONS, LLC

BICKERING BIRDS

Mildred Abbott

Cover, Logo, Chapter Heading Designer: A.J. Corza - SeeingStatic.com

Main Editor: Desi Chapman

2nd Editor: Corrine Harris

Recipe and photo provided by: Rolling Pin Bakery, Denver, Co. - RollingPinBakeshop.com

Visit Mildred's Webpage: MildredAbbott.com

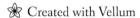 Created with Vellum

for
Nancy Drew
Phryne Fisher
and
Julia South

ABOUT BICKERING BIRDS

Rocky Mountain National Park has it all: rugged peaks, pine-scented forests, enchanting bird-watching locations, and... murder.

The Cozy Corgi bookshop finally opens, and Winifred Page and her headstrong corgi, Watson, are ready to welcome their first patrons. With her new best friend, Katie, creating heavenly pastries in the bakery on the top floor of the store, Fred's dreams are all coming together in delicious and unexpected ways.

When Katie caters a meeting of the Feathered Friends Brigade and drags Fred along, they expect nothing more than loquacious chatter about birds as they endeavor to build a professional relationship with the owner of the wild bird shop. Fred and Katie are quickly roped into a moonlight snowshoeing hike in hopes of spotting a rare owl. While the endangered bird proves elusive... the murdered man in the snow is hard to miss.

Fred's growing relationship with Sergeant Wexler hits a snag when he forbids her from donning her sleuth hat yet again. But Fred is a lot like her corgi—she doesn't like being told what to do, even if it puts an end to a possible romance.

As Fred and Watson delve into the lives of the ornithological club members, the tangled birds' nest of an investigation makes Fred wonder if she should have left this one to the police. But when feathers begin to fly, Fred has no choice but to flush out a killer...

ONE

"You can do this. You've been preparing for months. This isn't a big deal. You've done plenty of things much scarier." The reflection in the bathroom mirror squinted, obviously not believing the words. I couldn't blame her.

I shook my head, trying to clear it, and attempted to infuse my tone with more confidence. "You were a professor, started your own publishing company, and faced your crazy mother-in-law on your wedding day. This is nothing." The only thing the headshake accomplished was making my auburn hair frizz slightly so a strand became caught on my lip-gloss. I pulled it free. Leaning closer to the mirror, I sighed. A hunk of mascara was stuck in the corner of my eye. After retrieving a square of toilet paper, I fixed that without managing to mess up the half an hour of work I'd done on my face. I was tempted to wipe it all off. I hated wearing makeup, but I knew my uncle would comment if I arrived at my own opening night looking like it was just another day.

With another glare at my reflection, I thought I could hear the Winifred Page inside the glass whisper about how I left my years of teaching behind without looking back, got betrayed by my partner in our publishing company, and had been divorced for six years—negating any sense of accomplishment I might feel from those endeavors.

I straightened to my full five-ten height, squared my broad shoulders, and lifted my chin defiantly. "Well, maybe so, but I've solved two murders lately, and have successfully turned a run-down taxidermy shop into the most charming bookstore in the entire world. I've got this."

Before my mirror twin could offer further commentary, I threw open the bathroom door. In my haste, I nearly stepped on one of Watson's forepaws with my cowboy boots. He chuffed in annoyance but didn't bother to move. A corgi was the official breed of the Queen of England—I'd made the mistake of telling Watson that at some point, and clearly it had gone straight to his head. He was royalty, and he knew it.

"Sorry about that, buddy." I bent slightly and

ruffled the ginger fur between his ears. "Although I think it's your fault. You haven't been downstairs to see me once today. But if you're waiting for me outside the bathroom, it means you want something." I stepped around him and went to the main section of the bookshop, Watson's claws clattering over the hardwood floor behind me.

I paused, taking another breath. The sight of the Cozy Corgi finally complete did more to soothe my nerves than arguing with my reflection.

In the early January evening, night had fallen outside the large picture windows, and the gleaming hardwood floors, bookcases, and ceiling nearly glowed in comparison. The bookshop was laid out like a house, with a large center space surrounded by rooms and nooks around the perimeter. A couple of rooms had their own river rock fireplaces.

It was the bookshop of my dreams. Maybe I truly did have this.

A loud metallic clang sounded above the soft jazz piped in over the speakers, followed by muttered curses.

"Come on." I motioned to Watson but didn't bother to look back. "Let's go check on Katie. I'm pretty sure that's where you want me to go anyway."

I walked over to the large staircase in the center

of the space and headed upstairs. The appearance of the Cozy Corgi was as wonderful as I had imagined. The aroma of fresh-baked goodness wafted over the entire store—an aspect I'd neither planned on nor wanted, but it seemed like the icing on the cake, or the glossy cover on the book. Something....

In the weeks since Katie had decided to open her bakery on the top floor of my bookshop, the upstairs, originally an apartment, had been remodeled. A couple of walls had been removed, and most of the place was now open concept, with Katie's brand-new state-of-the-art kitchen glistening in all its shiny glass and stainless steel glory.

For a second, I didn't see Katie at the pastry-laden counter, but then her round face topped with her mass of curly brown hair popped up from behind. She let out a gasp. "Oh, Fred! You startled me." Her gaze traveled behind, landing on Watson. "I'm glad he was with you. I just dropped an entire tray of dog bones. If he'd been up here, he would've eaten all thirty of them before I had a chance to scoop them up." She laid a baking sheet piled with dog treats on the counter.

I glared down at Watson. "I knew there was a reason you came to see me. It wasn't for support, but permission."

Nonplussed, Watson trotted past me and plopped down in front of the bakery counter. It still amazed me that Katie had somehow managed to train him to not go into the cooking space. Although, I was certain the amount of baked bribery had something to do with it.

"I can't believe you took the time to make Lois's recipe for all-natural dog treats. It's opening night. The last thing you should be thinking about is Watson."

Katie scurried around the counter and tickled Watson's fox-like ears. "Don't say such a thing. The place is called the Cozy Corgi. Watson is the star."

By way of response, Watson lay, rolled over, and waited expectantly for Katie to rub his stomach.

She obliged.

Watson was one of the most reserved dogs I'd ever met, and there were few people he seemed to go crazy over. Katie wasn't one of the people he adored on principle, but he'd most definitely come to believe she was there to serve him.

"Do you mind if he has one?" She finished scratching Watson and stood, already reaching for one of the massive dog treat bones, certain of my response.

"Goodness knows I've come up here enough

times to sample everything you've done today. It would be rather hypocritical to deny him." I spared another glance around the space. Katie's bakery was a perfect match to the bookshop below. Somehow, she'd successfully blended old antique tables with rustic log chairs, and intermingled some of the spaces with overstuffed couches. Despite my claims to the mirror, I wasn't entirely sure I was prepared for my undertaking, but I was certain Katie was. I had no doubt she was born to be a baker.

"You doing okay?" Katie walked over to me, capturing my attention. "You look like you're going to be sick."

"Just nervous. But I'll be fine." I pulled out my cell from the pocket of my broomstick skirt and glanced at the time. "Five minutes. You ready?"

Katie squealed in way of response, threw her arms around me, and pulled me down into a hug. "This is going to be the best night ever!"

"Fred, darling, it's perfect. All of it. Absolutely perfect." Mom reached out and squeezed my hand. "It is you. It's just so you."

"That it is." My uncle, Percival, took me by my

shoulders and angled me toward him. "The question is, are you *you*?" He looked over at his husband, Gary, and widened his eyes. "We need to call that handsome sergeant Fred's been dating, let him know someone body-snatched our niece. This woman's wearing foundation and blusher."

Gary rolled his eyes and offered me his kind, bright smile. "You look lovely, Fred. But then again, you always do."

I shoved Percival off. "You are a pain. And I'm not dating Branson. We've only gone to dinner a couple of times."

Barry arrived as if out of thin air, waving one of Katie's ham-and-cheese croissants in the air. "Have you all had these yet? That woman is a miracle worker." My stepfather tore off a piece and tossed it to Watson, who was cavorting at his feet. Barry was one of the few my corgi truly did lose his mind over, even when food wasn't involved. "I left Zelda and Verona up there. I'm pretty sure they're clearing out everything Katie has in stock."

"I have to agree with you. Katie is a bit of a miracle worker. And that says a lot coming from someone who didn't even want a business partner up until a couple of weeks...." My brain caught up with my mouth, and I gaped at Barry before jerking the croissant out of his hands.

Though he looked surprised, Barry shrugged and grinned at me. "All you had to do was ask, love. You know what's mine is yours."

"No!" I shook the croissant at him. "This is her ham-and-cheese croissant. *Ham*, Barry! Ham!"

Mom sucked in a gasp, while Percival let out a near screech of a laugh, causing some of the customers milling about the bookstore to look over at us.

Barry plucked the croissant right back out of my hands. "Nope. She made a batch with meatless veggie ham slices, just for me."

"Oh, for crying out loud." Percival groaned and visibly deflated. "I thought we were finally putting an end to this vegetarian fad."

Mom gave a gentle slap to her brother's arm. "I think after twenty years, we can rest assured it's not simply a fad."

I let the comfort of their bickering fade away to background noise as I watched the people milling about the Cozy Corgi. There was a good turnout. Not only that, people seemed to be lingering. I'd feared they'd take one trip around the store and then leave. But people were spread out over the couches and chairs in all the different rooms, some of them eating Katie's pastries as they perused books.

My eyes stung, and I blinked away tears. Since I'd moved to Estes Park from Kansas City, there'd been several moments of confirmation that I'd made the right decision in hitting Reset on my life. This was another, and a significant one. With my family present, my dog at my feet, my new best friend baking her heart away up above me, and countless books around me, I was in heaven.

A squeeze on my hand made me glance over to meet Barry's watery blue eyes, which sparkled knowingly at me. He didn't need to say a word.

"I know you told Percival you're not dating the handsome sergeant, but I thought I might draw your attention to him walking through the door." Gary's low rumbling voice was warm against my ear as he leaned closer. "You'll probably want to greet him before he comes to us."

I let go of Barry's hand and winked in thanks at Gary. Lord knew what humiliating thing Percival would say if Branson Wexler walked over.

Though we'd been out two or three times over the past month, seeing him out of his police uniform still threw me off. At forty-two, and with the physique of a man a decade younger, Branson's handsome features were even more noticeable in his designer everyday clothes. He gave me a quick, warm hug and pressed his lips to my cheek. "Looks like you've got a smashing success on your hands, Fred."

Though pleased, I shrugged off the compliment. "They're mostly here for the baked goods." I could feel my family's gaze at my back. No chance Percival had missed that kiss. Percival *or* my mother.

"No false modesty needed here. You've bragged multiple times about being better at solving murder cases than half the police force, I'd think you could admit to making one stellar bookshop."

I nudged his chest playfully. "Brag? I don't brag." I pulled my hand away when I realized I was flirting. Good Lord. I was flirting. I cleared my throat. "You seriously do need to go upstairs and try Katie's baking before it's all gone."

"This won't be the last time I drop in, Fred." His green eyes gleamed, although maybe it was the reflection from the stained-glass lamp nearby. For a heartbeat, his expression faltered, and I thought he looked nervous, though that was an emotion I couldn't quite picture on Branson Wexler. It was gone almost as soon as it arrived, whatever it was. "I don't want to intrude if you have plans with the family, but I thought maybe I could take you out to a celebratory dinner when you're done. Maybe go back to Pasta Thyme?"

A mix of disappointment and relief flooded through me in equal measure. "I'm sorry, Katie and I are going to dinner afterward. But you read my mind. That's where we're going. I've been craving it ever since you took me there."

His eyes narrowed, playfully this time. "Well, I'm glad it's Katie you're going with. Otherwise I might get jealous of someone else eating with you at the place we had our first date."

"Oh, that's...." *Date!* He'd said date. Sure we'd gone out for dinners, but that was what we called it— going out to dinner. Not going out on a date. And we for sure hadn't labeled things as a first date or a second date. If that was what we were doing, then technically we'd had our third date a week ago. And granted, I hadn't been on a date in nearly fifteen years, but if what I remembered from third dates was still true, we most definitely hadn't been on one.

Branson's low chuckle brought me back to the moment. "You're rather ravishing when you're flustered, Fred Page."

Ravishing? I was many things, many good things, actually, but ravishing wasn't one of them. I'd never been *that* girl. And at nearly forty, I most definitely wasn't *that* woman. On good days, maybe I'd pass for pretty. But most of the time, I'd fall in the category of healthy and approachable.

Another laugh. "Yep. Being flustered is a great color on you."

As I tried to think of a response, any response, and in any possible language that would come out of my mouth, sensible or not, I glanced around the Cozy Corgi, seeking desperately for something to distract. When my gaze landed on it over Branson's shoulder, relief didn't begin to come close to what I was feeling.

And the it, wasn't an *it* at all. Leo Lopez walked through the front door of the bookshop. Unlike Branson, Leo was still in his uniform, clearly having just gotten off his shift at the Rocky Mountain National Park. The tan fabric of his park ranger outfit did nothing to hide his physique either, even with the bomber jacket he wore over it. Although, to be fair, his physique made more sense, as he was almost a decade younger than Branson. His brown eyes lit as his gaze landed on me, and he strode forward with a wide brilliant smile.

Probably noticing I'd been distracted, Branson turned, and at the sight of Leo, he stiffened.

For his part, Leo broke stride for a second, and

his smile transitioned from one of genuine beauty to something a little more forced. Unlike Branson, Leo didn't hug or kiss me when he joined us. "Congratulations, Fred. The place looks amazing, like I knew it would." He gave a slight nod of acknowledgment to Branson. "Wexler."

"Lopez." Branson returned the nod. If it had been any other two men, and any other situation, I would've laughed at the ridiculousness of them nodding oh so formally. It was such a male thing to do. Almost like two bighorn sheep I'd seen on a drive in the park the other day, each circling and measuring each other. With any luck, Branson and Leo wouldn't end the evening with a skull crushing head-butt.

Although, with the elevated tension, I wasn't entirely sure how true that would be.

"Thanks for coming by. So nice of you to take the time." I found my voice more out of desperation to break the moment than anything else.

It worked. Leo drew his attention back to me, the smile more genuine again. He pulled something out of his pocket, paused, and I could see the war raging internally. Then he held out a small box. "This is for your housewarming... er... grand opening." He cleared his throat, and I recalled Branson saying I was ravishing when I was flustered. Apparently that quality was going around. Leo shoved the box toward me. "It's not much."

"Thank you, Leo. You didn't need to do that." Impossibly, Branson stiffened even further as I took the gift. "I have no idea what the etiquette is for anything like this. Should I open it now?"

"Whenever you want." Leo shrugged. "Like I said, it's not much."

More to have something to do with my hands than anything, I pulled the thin red ribbon loose and lifted the small lid. Despite my internal promise to attempt to sound both pleased and neutral, I sucked in a genuine gasp of pleasure. I glanced up at him and then back to the silver earrings before lifting them into the air. Each one had three pounded-silver corgi silhouettes connected by tiny silver hoops. They glistened in the light.

Leo shrugged again. "I've noticed you really like dangly silver earrings." He motioned to the pair I had on. "I figure these are like them, except with little Watsons."

"I love them. They're perfect." I put them back in the box and closed the lid. "Thank you." I felt like I should hug him or something, but stayed where I was. Suddenly I prayed Barry would hurry over and say something ridiculous, no matter what it was. Or Percival, even if it was some horrid comment about me needing to choose between two handsome men. Or knowing Percival, telling me there was no reason to choose between two handsome men—that I should take them both.

And for crying out loud, Watson and I were here for mountains, family, and books—not men. I wasn't supposed to care about glistening green eyes or honey-yellow brown ones either for that matter. And I most definitely was not supposed to be stuck between two men, feeling awkward and self-conscious and oddly guilty—though I'd done nothing wrong—on the opening night of the Cozy Corgi. That wasn't the plan.

I slid the box into my pocket, then reached out with both hands and gave Leo's and Branson's forearms a quick squeeze simultaneously. "It is so wonderful for both of you to come. I simply can't thank you enough. However...." I glanced down at my feet, expecting to find Watson there, then remembered that Barry was nearby so I might as well be chopped liver. I saw the two of them exactly where I'd left them. Barry was lavishing affection on Watson, while the other three members of my family had been joined by Barry's daughters and their families.

The entire group was watching the fiasco that was my life. I slapped my thigh. "Watson. I promised you one of Katie's treats! I completely forgot."

At the word *treat*, Watson sprang to attention, and his gaze darted between Barry and me.

I might've smiled at Branson and Leo as I headed away, but I wasn't sure. I slapped my thigh again, this time hard enough it stung as I angled around my family and toward the stairs. "Come on, Watson. Treat!"

Thankfully the promise of a second of Katie's all-natural dog bones won out, and Watson headed in my direction.

Percival cocked an eyebrow as I slid past him, teasing thick in his tone. "Fred, I don't mind getting Watson his treat. I don't want to take you away from anything."

"Don't you dare." I offered him a glare and a shake of my finger, then made a hasty escape up the stairs.

True, I'd faced two different killers since my move to Estes Park the previous November. I knew some people considered me brave. Doubtlessly, that image would be shattered if they knew I was stuffing my face not simply because Katie was a master baker but because I was waiting for a farewell text from Leo or Branson. Honestly, I didn't care which one left. But I was certain neither would walk away without some sort of goodbye.

By the time I received Leo's parting message and braved returning downstairs, I'd devoured a ham-and-cheese croissant of my own—this one with ham from an actual pig—and polished off one of Katie's lemon bars for dessert. Never mind that the two of us were going to dinner in a matter of hours. Of course, Pasta Thyme had small portions, despite the expensive price tag, so I didn't feel too guilty about it.

Watson received another dog bone as payment for allowing me to use him as an escape. He opted to stay close to Katie as opposed to returning downstairs with me. I couldn't blame him.

I felt a little guilty but texted Leo back, thanking him again for the earrings.

He didn't respond.

I couldn't blame him for that either. I was the one who'd abandoned him. But it wasn't my fault both he and Branson had decided to pursue me for some stupid reason. Nor was it my fault they were both stupidly attractive and charming in their own ways. And it most definitely wasn't my fault my brain seemed unable to function properly when I was around either one of them.

Thankfully it was my family—and not Branson—who waited for me when I arrived on the main level. However, they were only waiting to say goodbye.

After watching them go, I glanced around, trying to spot Branson. I couldn't. Maybe I'd been wrong and he'd left without a farewell. I was okay with that too.

Relaxing somewhat, I wandered around the bookshop, chatting with customers. Most people didn't seem like they were there to buy anything, more to check out the grand opening of the Cozy Corgi. I knew part of the draw was coming into the place where Opal Garble was killed. That was fine. Book sales would come later. And even if they didn't, part of the blessings of being betrayed by my ex-business partner was ending up with enough money from the buyout that I could keep the bookstore running as long as I wanted. Provided I didn't develop some lavish lifestyle, including going to Pasta Thyme for too many dinners.

I fell more in love with my bookshop as I saw it through the eyes of those exploring it for the first time. I would change nothing about it. The lighting was perfect, the furnishings managed to strike a balance between well-crafted yet not ostentatious, and the entire environment truly was cozy. My affection for the bookshop continued to grow as I walked into my favorite section—the tiny room in the back left corner that I'd reserved for the mystery genre. It also happened to be the space with the largest river rock fireplace, which was little more than embers at the moment. And there was Branson, sitting on the ornate antique sofa, looking at a book by the light of a Victorian lamp.

The fact that I was relieved he hadn't left without a farewell betrayed my emotions. When I spoke, I was pleased my voice was steady. "What are you reading?"

He smiled up at me and presented the cover. *The New Exploits of Sherlock Holmes*. "Will you hate me if I confess I can't stand mystery novels?"

His statement took me aback, and I blinked. "You know.... Kinda, yes." I managed to laugh. "All right, maybe not *hate* you, but how in the world can anyone dislike mystery novels? Especially a police officer?"

He shrugged. "It's like being at work. Why would I want to read that? Spend all day solving cases, then come home to read about someone else doing it?" He shook the book. "Plus, Sherlock Holmes is a little bit arrogant, don't you think?"

"Give me that. You don't deserve to touch it." I snatched the book from his fingers, and though I managed another laugh, part of me was a bit offended for some reason. And in truth, my estimation of Branson Wexler went down a tick. My father had been the best policeman I'd ever met, and he'd devoured mysteries by the truckload. His favorite being all things Sherlock Holmes. "Surely you've realized you're in the mystery room. I'm not certain you even deserve to sit on the sofa or enjoy the fire."

"I stumbled on a land mine, didn't I?" He chuckled, and unless I was mistaken, heat seemed to glow in his eyes. "Although, I suppose I should know better. Your dog is named Watson, for crying out loud. Obviously you like Sherlock Holmes novels."

"Charlotte and I had done an open call for submissions for books similar to Sherlock Holmes at the publishing company right around the time Watson came into my life. It was kismet." And though Charlotte's and my business partnership had dissolved, Watson had lived up to his name on a couple of different occasions already.

"Well, he's pretty cute." He stood and lifted the book from my hand again. "I'll put this up for you. And who knows, maybe over dinner you can convince me about the charms of reading mystery novels." He flashed a hopeful smile, but it faded as something caught his attention over my shoulder.

I turned to see.

"Myrtle and her disciples." His voice was cold, more so than I'd ever heard it before.

I hadn't been sure what I was looking for, but at his words, I saw Myrtle Bantam. I was about to ask what he meant by *disciples*, and then figured it out. Maybe I didn't have my sidekick Watson with me, but I could put two and two together on my own at times. A crowd of people stood around Myrtle, each of them wearing rather hideous army green vests covered in various patches. I returned my attention to Branson. "You call the members of Myrtle's bird-watching club her disciples?"

He didn't look at me when he responded, keeping his narrowed eyes on the small group. "Yeah. They do her bidding. Drive the police force crazy, constantly accusing someone of poaching. It's every other week that there's a new suspect they're convinced has the police hoodwinked. Sometimes they turn in each other." He looked at me then, a partial smile returning. "She even has twelve of them. I'm not kidding."

Okay, even I had to admit that was a little funny. And I wasn't entirely surprised at Branson's reaction. Part of the conflict between him and Leo was because of Leo's insistence that the previous owner of my shop had been a poacher. Branson hadn't given his claims any credence, and Leo had been right.

"Do you mind if I leave this with you?" Branson handed the Sherlock Holmes book back to me. "And will you call me a coward if I request to escape through the back door? I don't have it in me to deal with that lot this evening."

Despite being relieved to see him, after our conversation about mystery novels, I was ready to see him go. It probably said horrible things about me that I would find someone wanting because they weren't in love with my favorite genre of literature. "Of course not. You know that Myrtle and I don't see eye to eye on everything either. And I appreciate you coming to the opening night. It is very sweet of you."

"Thanks for understanding." This time his smile was genuine, and he gave me another brief hug and a quick kiss on my cheek. "Congratulations, Fred. The Cozy Corgi is truly spectacular. See you soon." And with that, he was gone.

Time to focus on my bookshop and the potential customers instead of a love life that I didn't want to have anyway. Even so, at any other time, I would've had a similar reaction to Branson's at the sight of the bird club and go out of my way to check on other customers before going to Myrtle. It wasn't exactly bad blood between us, but she hadn't taken to me questioning the shop owners about murder when my stepfather had been accused. I'd kept my distance since then.

The group wasn't hard to find, nor were they in an unexpected place. There was another small nook, half of which was devoted to books about nature and wildlife, and the other half to photography. Steeling myself, I crossed the bookshop, smiling as I passed customers who caught my eye, and approached the group. Though not as tall as me, Myrtle was crane-like. She had a willowy figure, bordering on bony, and her white spiked hair was reminiscent of feathers. To top it off, she had a tendency to flap her arms when she spoke, and unfortunately also had a propensity to sound like she was squawking. She truly was bird in human form. The fact that she owned Wings of the Rockies, a wild-bird store, and led a bird-watching club, seemed the most natural thing in the world.

"Hi, Myrtle." I gave a little wave, feeling awkward as I drew closer. "And everyone else. So glad you all could come by the grand opening tonight." Two familiar faces caught my eye among her disciples—Branson's term of Myrtle and her ornithological friends truly did seem apt. "Carl, Paulie, I didn't know you two were members of the Feathered Friends Brigade." I scanned the other faces that turned in my direction. "Is Anna here?"

Carl grinned and hurried over to hug me. We'd never hugged before, but it seemed it was the thing to do at grand openings. I hadn't been aware of that fact. "No, she uses my time at the club as her girls' nights. She said to send her regards"—he pulled out a dog bone—"and to give Watson one of these." Carl and Anna owned the home furnishing store right across from the bookshop, and Anna was obsessed with Watson.

I took the dog bone. "Thank you. I'll make sure he gets it. Right now he's upstairs hoping to get more of Katie's baking, I'm sure."

"I'm the newest member. I joined recently." Paulie, who owned the pet shop, also gave me a hug. "Congratulations, Fred. The store is beautiful."

Carl gave me a knowing glance over Paulie's shoulder. "One of our members moved away, so we had an opening."

Paulie was relatively new to Estes Park and not very well liked. I was glad he was starting to find his place, maybe.

Myrtle cut off the greeting by thrusting a large hardback book in my direction. "Care to explain this?"

I took the heavy book out of her hand, instantly regretting my decision to come over. It seemed I was destined to make a bad impression on Myrtle, no matter what I did. I glanced at the cover. "Oh, yes. I remember ordering this one. Have you looked through it? The photographs are stunning. The bird-cages span the past two centuries. My favorites are the ones from the Victorian times." I pointed to the cover, which showed an example of just that. I caught Carl give a quick shake of his head, couldn't understand his meaning, and kept speaking. "There are some that look like entire homes, complete with rooms. Like genuine houses for birds."

"A genuine house for birds is a nest in a tree, Miss Page." As Myrtle's voice rose in volume, so did her propensity for sounding birdlike. A rather stunning pin of a swallow glinted on the scarf at her neck. "Unless, of course, you're talking about a belted kingfisher who uses holes in the ground, or the gyrfalcon that nests in the cliffs of the Arctic." She thumped the book with a bony finger. "I can promise you that none of them live in wire birdcages, especially ones designed to look like evil little houses. It's bad enough in regular cages, but in a contraption like that, there's not even a speck of room for a bird to spread its wings and fly more than an inch. Tell me, Fred, how would you like to live in such a torture device?"

I couldn't bring myself to look away from Myrtle, though I could feel the attention of the entire lower level of the shop staring at us. "I... honestly never thought of it like that. I suppose from that perspective, these cages aren't all that charming."

Myrtle stomped over to the shelf and pulled out

another book. She readjusted her peacock-feathered purse on her shoulder. "Now this one is appropriate. A bird-watcher's guide. If you manage to read it, it talks in length about the cruelty of domesticating birds." She smacked it on top of the other book. "Maybe you could take the time to read the books in your own store."

My temper flared, not entirely uncommon, but I managed to rein in my tongue before I said something I'd regret. *That* was unusual. I had to take a shaky deep breath before I allowed myself to respond. I'd promised myself I was going to do everything possible to make a good impression on the other storeowners of Estes Park; it seemed important we support one another. And if I had to eat crow to do it, I would. At least a little. "I don't have time right now, obviously, but if you'd like to arrange something later, maybe you could come down one evening and we could go through all the books on birds together. Let me know if there are some that might be harmful to birds, or make suggestions about others you think should be in here."

Once more I noticed Carl's eyes widen, and he gave an appreciative nod.

For her part, Myrtle's mouth fell open, and despite the tension of the moment, I couldn't help but think she looked like a young featherless bird in the nest hoping its mother would drop a worm in her gaping beak. Clearly she hadn't expected such a response.

Well, that made two of us.

"I will most definitely make time for that." Myrtle's voice had come back to a more reserved tone. "I very much appreciate your willingness to be educated on the subject." She smiled, the first one I'd ever seen from her. "Will tomorrow evening work?"

I started to shake my head, then envisioned another outburst. I wanted the town talking about the charm of my bookstore, and the perfection of Katie's delicacies when they mentioned the grand opening of the Cozy Corgi, not a screaming match between Myrtle Bantam and Winifred Page. And I supposed I might as well get the torture over with. "Tomorrow would be perfect."

Once again, surprise flitted across Myrtle's features, but she caught herself quicker this time. "Wonderful. See you then." Her gaze flicked to the door and then upstairs. "You know, it smells wonderful in here. Maybe the Feathered Friends Brigade should sample what little Katie is offering. Maybe we could start having pastries at our meetings."

There was a murmur of agreement from her disciples. And once more, proving I had a long way to go before I finally acted my age, they sounded like little chicks chirping after their mother hen. Even so, I appreciated the gesture. "That would be lovely." My grandmother's voice echoed in my mind, reminding me to kill my adversaries with kindness. "Please tell Katie when you go upstairs that everything your group has tonight is on the house."

"We'll do that." She gave a sharp nod, walked away, and lifted her hand over her shoulder and snapped her fingers. Sure enough, nearly as one, her disciples followed, Paulie giving a little wave as he passed.

There was one straggler who caught my arm and paused in place. "Don't let her push you around. Everyone thinks Myrtle Bantam is all about the environment, bird activism, and philanthropy, but I promise you, she's in it for the power. Nothing more."

I met the man's hard gaze. I hadn't seen him before. He was middle-aged and rather nondescript, but the anger in his eyes was almost alarming. "Well, I'm not sure about all that, but I know that I'm especially passionate about my corgi, and I assume Myrtle feels the same about birds." I considered myself a very good corgi mama, but I had no doubt I couldn't hold a candle to Myrtle's passion. Probably about anything.

He shook his head. "No. It's not about the birds. It's about power. The woman is an insane tyrant."

I couldn't imagine what power she got from leading a bird club, although she did seem in control of most of her members, but I had to admit she did seem a touch insane. I had no idea what to say to the man.

"Don't get on her bad side. I promise you. She'll—"

A large hand seemed to arrive out of nowhere and dropped onto the man's shoulder, silencing him. "Henry, would you care to join the rest of us for some pastries?"

I glanced toward the voice and met the gaze of another rather nondescript man, though I guessed this one to be around sixty as opposed to middle-aged. He smiled, lifted his hand from Henry's shoulder, and held it out to me. "I'm Silas Belle I don't think we've had the pleasure of meeting."

I shook his hand. "Nice to meet you. I'm Fred."

"I know. We're actually neighbors."

My little cabin was out in the woods, so much so that when I was in it, I felt the rest of the world had faded away. Then I remembered the new development of McMansions that had popped up on the road leading back into my woods. It was a stretch to call those my neighbors, but I supposed they were the closest thing I had to it.

For a second, it threw me off that Silas knew where I lived, but then I remembered that I was no longer in the city. In this small town, everyone knew everything about everyone else. Doubly true about the woman who moved into town, opened the bookshop, and helped solve two murders.

"Well, thanks for dropping by, *neighbor*." It was a silly thing to say, but at this point trying to find anything sensible seemed like entirely too much effort, or simply impossible.

"Anytime." Silas gave another smile, then turned to Henry. "Dessert?"

Henry flashed me a glance that said he hadn't been done ranting but followed as Silas led him away.

I watched them go. And to my relief, as they walked up the steps, Watson passed them on his way down. He spotted me as he reached the bottom and scurried over to be petted. Kneeling, I scratched both his sides, eliciting a small cloud of dog hair. "You knew I needed you, didn't you, buddy?" This night definitely had not gone how I'd envisioned. The bookshop truly was perfection, but.... People were much more complicated than any Sherlock Holmes book could ever be. Suddenly I couldn't wait to have a quick dinner with Katie and then go back home, light a fire, and read a book with Watson at my feet.

"Oh my goodness!" A loud screech caused Watson and me to stiffen, and I looked toward the voice. A large blonde woman towered over us. "This must be the corgi that your store is named after? Wilbur, right?"

"Watson, actually. From Sherlock Holmes. Wilbur was the pig in *Charlotte's Web*. Though, with the bakery upstairs, it's only a matter of time."

As the woman knelt to pet him, Watson shot me a glare. Maybe because he'd understood my jibe, or because I was clearly expecting him to allow a stranger to pet him. Or more likely, both.

Well, whatever. It was opening night, might as well make it awkward for both of us.

"Can you believe this? We've only been open for a hot minute, and I already have my first catered event." Katie beamed at me, and her excitement was so genuine I almost felt guilty for the negative things I'd been thinking. "And if they like them, maybe they'll have me do this every week. At least that's what Myrtle mentioned."

"Katie, there's no question they're going to like what you make. Your baking is perfect. Always." I shifted the large box of pastries to my other hand, managing to readjust the handle of Watson's leash without dropping anything as I reached for the front door to Wings of the Rockies. "My guess is that you'll get so many offers for catering events you're going to have to start turning them down."

Katie walked through, carrying twice as many pastries as me, a tweeting chime sounding overhead.

"You know, I'd be okay with that. I was already thinking I might need to hire an assistant."

I waited for Watson and then followed her through the door. I was about to say I'd been thinking the same thing about the bookshop, but my words fell away as thirteen faces turned to look at us. I'd been in Myrtle's shop once before, and it had been a mish-mash of birdfeeders, birdhouses, books, and countless things I couldn't identify. But it had seemed rather informal. Apparently that wasn't true on the nights the Feathered Friends Brigade met. The center of the space had been cleared, and rows of chairs had been set out, all facing a large pull-down screen. Myrtle stood in front, between the two rows of chairs, with her arms outstretched, having obviously been interrupted in midsentence.

Her gaze flicked to Watson, and her lips thinned.

The two of them hadn't exactly bonded the night before when Myrtle came to inspect my supply of bird books, but there hadn't been any open hostility either. From either of them. And things had gone smoother between Myrtle and myself than I'd antici-pated as well. I'd not even thought twice about having Watson tag along to the bird club. It seemed that had been an overestimation on my part.

If my hands hadn't been full, I would've checked

the time on my cell. "I'm so sorry! I was under the impression the meeting got started at seven." Katie and I had arrived with fifteen minutes to spare, or so I'd thought.

"We like to get started early." She motioned to a cleared spot on the counter close to the cash register. "If you'll place those there and then find a seat, we'll continue."

Katie and I arranged the pastries quickly and then looked toward the group. There were no chairs. The man from two nights ago stood, hurried over to a closet, and got two more folding chairs out for us. Surprisingly, I was able to remember his name by the time he brought them over. "Thank you, Silas."

"Of course! Glad you all can join us. It's rare we have visitors unless we're actively seeking enrollment."

"Which we're not. We are currently full." Myrtle gave what I thought was supposed to be a smile. "But we do consider it a part of outreach to have visitors. One never knows what might spark a passion for ornithology in someone." She waited for Katie and me to take our seats. "We were getting ready to start the awarding of badges. It's always one of the first orders of business." I could quite literally see her debating how much she wanted to explain. It seemed

Myrtle was feeling gracious, or maybe she and I had bonded more than I'd realized the night before. "We have five categories for which members compete for honors." She numbered them off on her fingers as she listed the categories. "Having experiences with the rarest bird, with photographic evidence of course, while obviously not infringing upon the bird's space. Capturing sounds of rare birds. Having raised the most money for conservation for the week. Demonstrating impressive ornithological knowledge. And an adept ability at replicating birdcalls without the aid of electronic assistance."

"I always get that one!" Carl grinned and waved a chubby hand in our direction, earning himself a glare from Myrtle.

Myrtle cleared her throat. "If we're done with interruptions, I assume it's safe for me to commence." She didn't wait for a response. "Did anyone travel this week and have any images to share with the club?"

"Like we don't already know." The mutter was low enough that I thought I was the only one who heard, and I dared to look over. Henry met my gaze and rolled his eyes.

"I spent a couple of days last week traveling over southern Australia." Silas stood and walked toward the front, handing Myrtle a flash drive. He continued speaking as she put it into her laptop. She clicked a few buttons and an image of a little green bird with blue wings appeared on the screen. "The orange-bellied parrot was quite captivating, so much so that I nearly extended my stay simply to spend more time watching it in its natural environment."

The quiet groan to my right at Silas's announcement was once again too quiet for most to hear, and I didn't need to look over to see that Henry was having another reaction.

"Don't forget to announce what camera you used to capture that image, Silas." A handsome younger man spoke from Katie's left.

Silas let out a good-natured laugh. "Of course, Benjamin. For this trip, I took my Nikon D500 DSLR. It did a perfect job, as you can see."

Benjamin halfway stood, addressing the club. "Remember that all members of the Feathered Friends Brigade get ten percent off all camera equipment at my store."

"Benjamin! We've talked about this. I'm not running an advertising group here." Myrtle's lips thinned further to a near birdlike point, and then she motioned to Silas. "Sorry for the interruption, please continue."

Silas began listing different facts about the orange-bellied parrot as well as details about where he stayed for his two days in Australia. Katie leaned close to me, her curly hair tickling my cheek as she whispered, "He traveled all the way to Australia and only stayed two days? Who can afford that?"

Myrtle cleared her throat and cast a glare in our direction. I didn't respond to Katie, she obviously hadn't noticed the gathering of mini-mansions on the way to my house. From the looks of them, several of the occupants could afford such a trip. Especially those whose mansions weren't all that mini. At the end of his speech, once Myrtle was assured no one else had any images to share that they thought might outdo Silas's, she handed him a brightly colored badge. It seemed to match at least ten other badges already affixed to his vest.

Next came the badge for captured sounds. A middle-aged woman named Alice also handed Myrtle a flash drive, and then a moan-like chirp filled the space. She too gave a little speech about whatever bird was making the noise, but instead of listening, I was distracted once more by Henry's reaction. Making sure Myrtle's attention was fixed on Alice, I glanced around the group. It seemed Henry wasn't the only one annoyed. And when Alice was awarded a different badge, judging from her vest, it was once again clear she was a common recipient of that particular achievement. As she spoke, it seemed obvious she wasn't as confident in her facts as Silas had been. I couldn't help but wonder if Alice was cheating somehow, though I couldn't imagine Myrtle allowing such a thing to occur in her club.

A man named Owen won the badge for raising the most money for bird conservation over the previous week. It was the second badge on his vest. Even so, Henry let out another quietly disgusted sound. The man seemed to despise everyone in the club. It didn't make any sense for him to be there. I dared another glance. There were no badges on his vest.

"Now for my favorite part of the evening, we will see if anyone can earn the badge for knowledge of our feathered friends." Myrtle clicked a few buttons on her laptop, before diving into her first question.

Beside me, Katie shifted in her seat in apparent anticipation.

"We'll start with an easy one." As she spoke, Myrtle's voice took on the tone of the teacher and sounded the least birdlike I'd ever heard from her. "True or false, an ostrich sticks its head in the sand because of fright."

Before anyone could respond, Katie's hand shot up into the air so hard that she nearly threw herself from the chair.

Myrtle flinched, her eyes widening. She swallowed, like she was debating what to do, and then she offered a forced smile. "Normally nonmembers don't participate, as they are not eligible to win badges, but we'll make an exception this time. What say you, Miss Pizzolato?"

"That is false."

Myrtle's smile turned a little more genuine. "You are correct. Although that is a fairly sensible response. In truth—"

"They stick their head in the ground to look for water."

I turned to gape at Katie, shocked and a little impressed that she'd interrupt Myrtle Bantam. It was like being back in grade school and the class know-it-all dared to correct the mean substitute teacher.

For her part, Myrtle didn't seem offended in the least. "Very true! I must say I'm impressed. Though the next won't be quite so easy." She checked her computer screen. "The bassian thrush has an unusual way of—"

Katie's hand shot in the air again, this time causing Myrtle to look annoyed. "They use flatulence to lure out their prey. They aim at where they suspect the worms will be and... well... fart...." Katie blushed. "It disturbs the worms, causing them to make their location known."

Myrtle blinked, and several of the members turned to stare at Katie.

Almost begrudgingly, Myrtle nodded. "True enough. Although in the future, I appreciate being able to finish the question." She didn't wait for a response before launching into the next. "There's a bird that dyes its feathers, much like many of you dye your hair—" She flinched as Katie's hand jutted skyward once more, but kept going. "They do this by staining their feathers with red mud. What is this particular bird species?"

Katie waved her hand, and Myrtle looked around at the other members of the club, clearly hoping one of them would save her. No one did. With the sound of defeat, she gave a nod in Katie's direction. "Yes, Miss Pizzolato?"

"It's the lammergeier, more commonly known as the bearded vulture. And it doesn't start that particular behavior until around the age of seven years old."

Everyone, me included, gaped at Katie.

She shrugged. "Well, they do."

Just as I was wondering what other levels of savant knowledge my new best friend possessed, I realized what had happened. As Myrtle checked her screen again, I leaned into Katie. "You entered the Google wormhole about birds last night, didn't you?"

She looked at me like that was the dumbest question anyone had ever asked. "Well, of course I did. I knew we were coming here. I wanted to be informed."

I loved that Katie was such a peculiar woman at times.

"This is our final question. I must say, I'm curious if any of the actual Feathered Friends Brigade will be able to get anything correct this evening, or if you all will be shown up by our caterer." Seeming a little shaken, Myrtle sighed. "This particular species is being driven almost to extinction through poaching because of its red ivory bill." She didn't bother to look surprised as Katie's hand shot up again. Although she did seek the faces of her club members with a desperate expression. Finally her gaze landed on Silas. "Surely you know this."

"I believe I do, yes. But I'm fascinated." Silas nodded but smiled at Katie. "Tell us, Katie. Can you prove to be as much of an expert on birds as you are at baking?"

This time, Katie's cheeks were a vibrant red as she spoke. "It's the helmeted hornbill. And on the black market, their beaks are more expensive than elephant ivory."

"Well done!" Silas clapped, and within a couple of moments, the rest of the group joined in.

Katie looked like she was in heaven.

"She's cheating. Her friend is looking things up on the phone and whispering to her." Henry stood, glaring at Katie and me in something akin to hate. "You two will fit in perfectly here."

To my surprise, both Carl and Paulie stood up, but it was Paulie who spoke first. "Fred would never do that! She's the most honest and kindest person I know. There's been no one in town who's been nicer to me than her."

Guilt cut through me at his words. I did consider myself fairly honest, but I hadn't always had the kindest thoughts about Paulie.

Myrtle clapped her hands, surprisingly able to make quite a loud noise, considering how thin and bony they were. "None of this! Not in my club. Ever!" She pointed at Henry. "Keep yourself under control, or I will expel you from the club and we will have an opening after all. I will not warn you again."

Henry turned every bit as red as Katie had

moments before, looking like he was about ready to burst, but then, to my surprise, sat down and clasped his hands together in his lap.

Myrtle glared at him a few extra seconds, then motioned for Katie to come forward. "As I said, nonmembers are excluded from earning badges, but —" She unfastened a pin similar to the ones I'd noticed her wear the past two nights, this one in the shape of a hummingbird. "—take this."

"Oh no, I can't. That's much too nice. I wasn't trying to win anything."

Myrtle thrust the pin into Katie's hand. "I insist. And the next time we have an opening in the club"— she cast a quick glare at Henry—"you have a standing invitation to join."

Katie squeezed back into the seat beside me, most uncomfortable. "I was trying to enjoy the quiz. I wasn't attempting to cause drama."

"I know. There seems to be some other dynamic going on here besides you being good at trivia."

Myrtle cleared her throat, casting an annoyed glare in my direction, and then continued. Next came the badge for birdcalls. I inspected Katie's new pin as multiple people stood and made strange noises. I was thankful for the distraction of the pin as I found it rather embarrassing to hear adults attempting to sound like birds. As for the pin, it was beautiful—and obviously expensive. The casing was silver, and the details were crafted in a mosaic of glossy stones. Myrtle must truly have been impressed to offer such a reward. By the time I handed the pin back to Katie, Carl was accepting his badge for the best birdcall of the evening.

The rest of the meeting was entirely comprised of what equated to be a sermon from Myrtle. And if I hadn't already been convinced, Branson's descriptor of the group as Myrtle and her disciples, was proven accurate. She spoke with as much fervor about conservation, ending poaching, and being on guard for the signs of it in and around Estes and the national park, as any sermon of fire and brimstone I'd ever witnessed, not that I'd heard that many.

As she spoke, I studied the twelve members of the group, trying to understand why they were there. I couldn't see the appeal, they seemed like they had signed up to be led by a dictator, one who liked to hear herself speak. Henry's words came back to me from two nights before—claiming that Myrtle was power-hungry. From what little I'd seen, I couldn't disagree with him, despite her generosity toward Katie. But that made it even more confusing. Henry clearly didn't like what was going on in the group. I thought his annoyance had mainly been directed at Myrtle, but it seemed to be at nearly everyone in the club. So why be a member at all?

From what I knew about Paulie, it made sense, sad as it was. He was hard to be around and awkward to an extreme. As a result, he was desperate for relationships. I wasn't surprised he would be willing to put up with nearly anything to try to fill that void. But the rest, I couldn't imagine. Carl was a little odd to be sure, but he and Anna were the center of the gossip chain in Estes Park. He wasn't lacking for friendships. I didn't know any of the other members personally, maybe most of them were lonely like Paulie, or maybe they were genuinely passionate about birds. I supposed they would have to be to sit through something like this on a weekly basis.

Personally, I couldn't fathom it. Even if the group was about corgis, or specifically about Watson, for crying out loud, I would never subject myself to such an experience more than once.

Myrtle must have some odd draw or power I couldn't see. Something more than badges about birds was going on here. Surely.

The meeting ended, and everyone gathered around the pastries, bragging about Katie's skills, with equal measure of her bird knowledge. Several of them came up to me to give Watson attention. I was impressed with his begrudging willingness to allow all the strangers to fawn over him. My poor little guy was getting used to it after the few days at the bookshop. When there was a break in the attention, Henry made his way over to us. I might have been willing to play nice on the opening night of the Cozy Corgi, but I wasn't going to do that again, and I prepared to tell him so. To my surprise, he grimaced as he approached, and he gave an apologetic shrug. "I'm sorry, Miss Page. Sometimes my temper gets the better of me. I'm so used to people cheating in order to get badges that I jump to conclusions."

I looked around expecting to see some other member over his shoulder having encouraged him to apologize, like a mother would to a child. There was no one. "Thank you, Henry. I appreciate it. And I can promise you that neither Katie nor I cheated. Katie's simply especially fond of trivia, of any variety. Give her five minutes on any topic, and she'll become an expert it seems. It's a skill I can assure you I don't have."

Henry nodded and seemed unsure what to say. Then he appeared to steel himself and met my gaze.

"If the rumors are true, you have a good relationship with Sergeant Wexler, is that right?"

I could tell we were heading into dangerous territory. "I'm new in town, so I'm getting to know a lot of people at the moment. But Bran—Sergeant Wexler and I have a lot in common. My father was a policeman."

He nodded like that made sense. "That's great. Maybe you can get him to listen to us sometimes. He refuses to follow up on any leads we offer about people we know are poaching."

It took all my willpower to refrain from pointing out that he'd just accused Katie and me of cheating at a trivia game. It seemed a little much to expect a policeman or anyone else to give him much credence. "If that's happening, it's awful. Maybe it's something Leo Lopez can help you with." Even as I said it, I felt guilty for throwing Leo under the bus. "Do you know him? He's a park ranger."

"Yes, he's one of the good guys. He doesn't always take us seriously either, but more than anyone else." His eyes lit. "In fact, he's leading us on a moonlight snowshoe next week in hopes of spotting some owls. You should attend."

I couldn't imagine anything I would rather do less than attend another meeting of the Feathered

Friends Brigade. "I doubt that will work out. Having opened the bookshop, I'm afraid every ounce of my time is spoken for."

Henry looked disappointed, though I couldn't imagine why. "Well, if you change your mind, bring Katie along. I'm sure Myrtle will allow you to attend as long as she's there. But don't bring your dog." He cast a disapproving glance at Watson. "Although I suppose I shouldn't tell you to bring Katie. Clearly Myrtle would like nothing more than to kick me out and put her in."

Even though I knew it was rude, I couldn't keep from asking. "Henry, I hope you don't mind me saying so, but you seem rather miserable here and as if you don't like a lot of the people in the club."

He shrugged.

I took that as an agreement. "Then why attend?"

Some of the heat returned to his voice, though I couldn't tell if it was anger or merely passion. "Despite what others might think, the Feathered Friends Brigade is not about the badges, taking trips to see fancy birds, or making friends. It's about protecting nature, about rescuing species of birds on the edge of extinction, about raising money for conservation. About making the world a better place." He leaned closer, his voice barely more than a whisper. "And there is a saying about keeping your friends close and your enemies closer. That's exactly what I'm doing. And I will get the Feathered Friends Brigade back on track and weed out those who corrupt what it stands for. Even if I have to take down Myrtle to do it." He nodded and pointed a finger in my face, almost hitting my nose. "Mark my words, I'm going to expose the people in this club for exactly what they are, the cheaters, those who don't care about the birds at all, and even the poachers among us."

Over the next week, two things became clear.

The most important was that Katie and I needed to hire at least one person apiece. Even though the winter was the slow season, neither of us could keep up. Granted, I had it easier than Katie. At most, I simply needed to step into the restroom and leave customers unattended for a few moments. She had to get up at four in the morning to begin baking and then serve customers all day. She was wearing herself out.

The other thing was that attending the Feathered Friends Brigade had stoked Katie's competitive side. Between discussing new ideas for recipes and attempting to use inspiration from the literary themes in the bookshop, Katie talked incessantly of wanting a vest filled with trivia badges. I wasn't entirely certain if the sleep-deprived bags under Katie's eyes were due to how hard she was working at the bakery or how long she spent on Google before going to bed.

Katie's new obsession, combined with a text invitation from Leo, had me strapping on snowshoes for the first time in my life. Under the moonlight, as snow drifted down, I couldn't help but envy Watson his coziness and warmth back home. He'd made it very clear as I left him behind that he was irritated, but little did he know he was getting the better end of the bargain.

Leo led the fifteen of us through the moonlit forest over a relatively flat and easy trail that led to Bear Lake before pausing at the water's edge to turn and address the group in a low voice that carried without disrupting the serenity. "I know I don't have to tell any of you this, but as we split up, stay with your buddy, and remember to be as still as possible. The chances of spotting any nocturnal birds while we're tromping around is low, but especially so if we're talking."

I let his words fade away, distracted as a cloud

moved above and moonlight washed over his features. He made quite the picture in his park ranger uniform, bomber jacket, and fleece hat and gloves, standing in front of the iced-over lake, snow-covered mountains at his back, and winter forest surrounding him. He looked utterly comfortable and totally capable. I'd been a little surprised at his text, especially after the way I'd abandoned him on the opening night of the Cozy Corgi. Part of me had wondered if Katie had put him up to it—one more nail in the coffin to get me to attend. If she had, it worked. His invitation had been the deciding factor.

"Again, I know none of you need to hear this, but I'll say it anyway. No flash photography. It disturbs the wildlife. And I know everyone's hoping to see a Mexican Spotted Owl, but as you know, they tend to stay in the southern parts of the Rocky Mountain National Forest. Only occasionally will they wander this far north."

That particular species had been the reason Leo and I had first met, when I'd found a frozen owl in the deep-freeze of the shop. It ended up being the proof Leo had needed that the previous owner had been involved in poaching. Although, considering he was already dead, it was too little, too late.

Leo tapped his watch. "We will meet back here in an hour. Reception at this location is decent, and each of you has my cell number. Call me if there's any problem. If all else fails, shout." He flashed a brilliant grin. "Good luck!"

The members of the Feathered Friends Brigade dispersed, all nearly silent. I supposed that was a prerequisite for adequate bird-watching. Leo nodded at Myrtle as he passed her and headed to Katie and me. "How are you two doing? Neither of you have snowshoed before, correct?"

"It's not too bad." Katie shrugged. "I did some research about snowshoeing last night and found a website that suggested different stretches to help get ready. I'm feeling pretty good."

I threw my arm around her shoulders and gave her a quick squeeze. "Of course you did."

Leo chuckled but then turned his attention to me. "And you? I imagine these mountain winters are hard to get used to."

"I can't say I'm used to the elevation yet or hiking in the middle of the night through snow, but as far as the cold, it's not nearly as intense as Kansas City."

"Good. I'm glad you're adjusting." He looked a little nervous. I knew how he felt. We'd already resorted to talking about the weather. "Do you two want to go off and search the woods on your own, or would you like me to accompany you?"

Before Katie or I could respond, Henry hurried over and grabbed Leo by the arm, and though he attempted to whisper, temper was clear in his tone, and his words certainly carried. "I'm glad I caught you without the others around. I was wrong before. About Roxanne." He cast a glance at Katie. "She was the trivia queen, at least before you showed up." Without waiting for a response, he turned back to Leo. "She isn't the poacher. It's Owen. I'm sure of it this time."

"Okay, Henry." Though Leo sighed, his tone was patient. "Let's do like we have every time before. This isn't the place for it. Give me a call tomorrow, and I'll listen to whatever proof you think you have."

"*Think* I have?" Henry's whisper turned to a hiss. "Don't you start acting like that cop. Already making up your mind about me before you've even heard what I have to say. I don't *think*, Leo. I *know*." He gave Leo's arm a shake. "And I know that Owen is the poacher."

Proving she was as adept at moving silently as a park ranger, Myrtle suddenly joined our group, fury visible in her eyes, despite the night shadows. "Enough of this, Henry. You've got to quit accusing people in the group of poaching. We are all on the same side. Every one of us is committed to protecting our birds. All of us. I'm not going to continue to have this conversation with you."

"Oh yes, Myrtle, queen of us all." All attempt at whispering left Henry's voice. "You like to pretend you're all high and mighty, so perfect. But you know about the cheating that goes on. And yet you continue to give badge after badge after badge. While those of us who actually play by the rules get nothing. Like anyone can trust anything you say."

"How dare you speak that way about Myrtle." During the exchange, I'd not noticed Silas at Myrtle's side. And though he did whisper, there was no wavering in his voice. "Do you know how much this woman has done for conservation, how much money she's raised? Where would any of us be without her? How can you even suggest that—"

Myrtle raised her hand, quickly touching his arm. "Thank you, Silas, but I can defend myself." She addressed Henry, and for once there was no birdlike squawk to her voice. It was cold, hard. "I'm done with warnings, Henry. *You're* done. You're out of the group. As soon as we get back tonight, hand in your vest. Your membership is suspended."

Henry had murder in his eyes. "Of course, Myrtle. Three weeks after membership fees are collected. After you make clear that ten grand is nonrefundable, now you kick me out? You've been looking for a reason." He laughed as he ripped off his vest and threw it at Myrtle's face. "You are a piece of work. And I'll bring you down. I promise you that."

Silas took a step toward him, but Myrtle shot out her arm once more, stopping him.

Henry whirled and headed into the forest.

Leo reached for him. "Henry, calm down. It's not safe to go out there by yourself right now."

"I'm as adept in these woods as you are." Henry shook him off. "And you're as bad as she is. Already making up your mind that you know better than me. Mark my words. Owen is the poacher. I'll prove it."

As Henry stormed off, Leo started to follow him, but Myrtle stopped him. "Let him go. Henry is wrong about many things, but he can take care of himself. And from the outbursts I've already seen from him, following will make things worse. For both of you."

Leo hesitated, glanced down at the solitary trail

in the snow that led to where Henry headed, then gave a slow nod. "You're probably right."

Without any more concern in her tone, Myrtle turned and addressed Katie. "There's an opening in the Feathered Friends Brigade. It's yours if you want it."

"I... um...." Katie looked at Henry's footprints, then back at Myrtle. "Um... membership is ten thousand dollars?"

"Yes." Myrtle nodded. "Annually, of course."

"Oh, yes, naturally." Katie licked her lips. "May I... let you know?"

"Certainly, dear." Myrtle gestured toward the forest. "I'm going to attempt to find my first Mexican Spotted Owl this evening. Wish me luck." She and Silas headed out.

Once the pair was out of earshot, Katie turned to face Leo and me, her expression aghast as she met my gaze and then Leo's. "Ten thousand dollars? A year! As if that makes any difference. It wouldn't matter if it were that much for the rest of the century. Who has that kind of money?"

"Well, it is Estes Park. Half of the residents are stinking rich, and the other half of us barely scrape by." Leo shrugged. "However, in this case, I'm thankful for the fee. Every dime of it goes toward preventing poaching. And not just for birds."

That price tag was rather astounding and unexpected. And while I didn't fall into the barely scraping by category, I couldn't imagine paying ten thousand dollars to be in any kind of club, even if the proceeds did go to a worthy cause.

"Well, that part is good, I suppose." Katie grinned at me as she shook her head. "I no longer want a vest filled with bird trivia badges." She slipped her arm through Leo's. "Lead on, Smokey Bear."

Leo let out a guffaw, and somehow managed to still stay quiet. "New nickname?"

"Not overly original as far as names for park rangers go, I know. But whatever." Katie linked her other arm through mine. "Come on. If we have to be out in this godforsaken cold without the hope of getting any badges, the least we can do is enjoy a private tour. Make it interesting, Smokey."

Leo didn't attempt to make it overly interesting. He didn't need to. He filled in some quiet facts here and there, but mostly, he let Mother Nature speak for herself. He led us through the trees, twenty yards or so away from where we'd been, before he stopped and smiled at us. "Now, listen. Don't move anything besides your head. Listen and watch."

Katie giggled but settled in quickly enough.

After a minute or so, I nearly forgot the two of them were there. I'd visited Estes Park since I was a kid, seeing my mom's family a couple of times a year. But somehow, I'd forgotten exactly what the Colorado mountains were like. Even with the brightness of the full moon, with the clarity of the air and sky, the swirls of the starry galaxies above our heads twinkled down upon us, mystical against the dark silhouettes of the trees and the craggy peaks that surrounded us.

In the silence, the night came alive. A soft wind swept cold fingers across my cheek and dislodged some snow that had piled up on the leafless branch of an aspen, causing it to tumble down like a waterfall. The crackle of underbrush sounded close to my feet, though I couldn't see anything, not even the trembling of the undergrowth.

My eyes continued to adjust, helped along by the reflection of the moon over the snow, allowing me to see farther through the dense forest, illuminating boulders scattered among the trees.

A louder rustling sounded to our right. I turned to look, expecting to see one of the members of the

Feathered Friends Brigade. Instead a bull elk stared at me from less than thirty feet away, its seemingly limitless pointed antlers forming a crown above its head. On its own, the sight wasn't that unusual. The elk in Estes Park were nearly as tame as dogs, often wandering through the main streets. But as glorious as that was, it didn't compare to seeing the majestic creature in its kingdom, undisturbed by other people. It huffed a steaming breath and then moved on, only then did I notice another five or six farther back in the trees.

Katie let out a quiet contented sigh. I agreed wholeheartedly.

I'd traded my old life for one filled with books, family, and magic. I hadn't expected that last one.

A high-pitched scream cut through the night, breaking the spell. The heads of every elk straightened, and then as one, they disappeared into the trees.

A second scream split the air. Leo, Katie, and I exchanged a brief glance, then like the elk, moved as a unit, though we ran toward the sound.

As we moved, we could hear others running through the forest, all headed in the same direction as us.

No more screaming came, but as we drew closer,

we were led by the sounds of a woman close to hyperventilating.

We entered a small clearing and saw Alice and an older woman standing over a dark shape on the ground.

A few steps closer, and thanks to the moonlight, the snow, and my adjusted eyesight, the dark shape took form. Henry lay on his back. His eyes stared sightlessly up into the trees. A gaping wound sliced across his neck.

Though they were always helpful when I needed to know something, I had to admit, I'd at times thought judgmental things about Anna and Carl and their propensity for gossip. Sometimes even about my uncles as well. Within half an hour of opening the Cozy Corgi the next morning, I was taking back every negative thought I'd had. You didn't have to go looking for gossip as a storeowner; it came to you. And judging from the vast number of people wandering through the bookshop to head upstairs to Katie's bakery and how few were returning back down, I had the feeling we were going to be the new hub.

Once more thinking I needed to bring on an employee to handle the cash register, I left my post and wandered up to the bakery, Watson following grudgingly along.

I had to eat my words about Watson as well. I would've been willing to bet everything I owned on him never being back in the bookstore again once the bakery was in full swing. I'd not taken into account the vast number of people who would linger in the charming space Katie had created. It turned out that as much as Watson adored food, he valued avoiding countless hands on him even more. He was always underfoot in the bookshop. Which, I had to admit, pleased me greatly.

Katie noticed Watson and me arriving at the top of the stairs, and she cast me a wide-eyed glance before turning back to her customer. I hadn't quite grasped how many people had not yet come back down to the bookshop. The place was filled. Though there weren't many, every table, sofa, and chair were occupied, and people huddled in little groups whispering excitedly.

I started toward the counter, but then, to my surprise, noticed Carl gesturing emphatically a few feet away. He must've felt my gaze as he looked over at me at that exact moment, brightened, and waved me over before turning back to his audience. "Ask Fred, she was there. Henry lay there in the snow, throat sliced open like in a horror movie."

I started to confirm, but felt strange about it, so I

changed directions. "Carl, what are you doing here? I can't believe Anna allowed you to leave her by herself in Cabin and Hearth."

He looked at me like I was an idiot, then gestured across the bakery. "She's getting us another tart. We saw everyone coming over here, so we closed the shop. Didn't want to miss the excitement."

Apparently I hadn't completely misjudged Carl and Anna's propensity for gossip after all. And strangely, that felt soothing.

As if hearing her name, Anna shuffled over and shoved a plate with the pear tart toward Carl, then plunged a fork into her slice of chocolate cake. She smiled at me, glanced down, then returned the fork to the plate with a clatter and shoved it in my direction. "Hi, Fred, hold this." She sank to the floor, her gingham skirt billowing around her as she squealed and reached toward Watson.

I swore he grimaced, but he knew one of his favorite treat dispensers when he saw her and allowed the fawning to happen.

Carl took a bite of his tart and groaned in pleasure, then gestured over his shoulder with the fork toward Katie, speaking with his mouth full. "You landed a goldmine with that one, Fred."

"That I did."

"I'm betting it's a matter of weeks before you put the Black Bear Roaster out of business."

I grabbed his arm. "Don't say that! We are not in competition with the coffee shop. There is enough business for both of us." The Black Bear Roaster had been the only coffee shop downtown until Katie opened. The owner wasn't my favorite person in the world, and she couldn't serve a moist scone to save her life, but I didn't want that notion of us trying to put them out of business to start getting around town.

With a final pat on Watson's head, Anna stood and retrieved her cake. "Don't be ridiculous. Of course you're in competition with Carla. And you're going to knock her socks off."

"No! I don't want—"

"So what's your version, Fred?" Anna cut me off with her mouth as full as Carl's. "I'd say you'll have a much calmer account than my husband. This is the first time he's seen a murder. By this point, it's got to be almost boring to you. I swear, you moved to town, and people start dropping like flies."

The couple Carl had been talking to nodded enthusiastically. I didn't believe I'd met them before, but I offered an uncomfortable smile. "I... ah... don't know if I would put it like that exactly. And...." I glanced over Carl and Anna's shoulders and pointed toward Katie as I raised my voice. "Of course, I'll be right there." I tried another smile, this time at Carl and Anna. "Sorry, Katie needs me. Enjoy your breakfast." Without worrying if I had been convincing or not, I headed toward the counter, even though Katie hadn't even been looking in my direction.

Katie noticed me when I was a couple feet away and grinned. "Perfect timing. Fred, I want you to meet Sammy." A short woman turned to offer me a greeting, a broad smile on her round face, and I halted. I could've been looking at Katie's twin, or at least her sibling. They even had the same mess of curly brown hair. "Sammy is a baker. She graduated culinary school at Christmas and came home to spend a few months with her family. I'm trying to talk her into being my assistant. Even if only for a few months until we get settled."

I shook the woman's hand. "Nice to meet you. It would be great to have Katie get some help. I need to start looking for some myself."

"Nice to meet you, too. Absolutely love your bookstore. It's wonderful." Sammy broke the handshake and attempted to trap a curl behind her ear, it sprung free the second she dropped her hand. "And from the looks of things, I'll be getting a great experience. You're crazy busy."

She even sounded like Katie. It was a little disconcerting. "Well, that's true, but I'm willing to bet it'll die down after a day or two. People are excited or something after last night's events."

"Are you kidding?" Katie scoffed. "With you around, the adventure never stops. Give us another few weeks and eventually you'll find another dead body."

"Not you, too!" I think for the first time in our friendship I gave her an irritated glare. "This doesn't have anything to do with me. And you were with me, remember? Neither of us discovered Henry's body. That was Alice, and...." I snapped my fingers trying to remember the other woman's name. "Lucy."

Katie shrugged, like that was a minor detail. Then she turned back to Sammy. "Just wait and see. Give Fred a week and she'll be able to tell the whole town who killed Henry. She's the best detective the town's got."

I wondered if Anna and Carl would loan me the key to their store so I could hide in there for a while. "Katie, don't be ridiculous. I own a bookshop. I'm not a detective. There's no reason for me to get involved in this. None of my family or friends have been accused of murder."

Again Katie waved me off like I was being ridiculous and somewhat daft. "Like that matters."

I wasn't about to admit I'd had similar thoughts as I'd fallen asleep the night before. Playing over the interactions I'd noticed at the bird-club meeting, it wasn't hard to imagine half of those people wanting Henry dead. It seemed like I'd heard him accuse most of the bird-watchers of some form of foul play. That probably got a little old, to say the least. I hadn't noticed anything interesting about Owen, but I doubted he felt too kindly toward Henry after being accused of poaching.

I gave my head a shake, clearing the ridiculous things I was thinking. But too little, too late. Katie shook her finger in my direction and grinned. "I know that face, Fred." She winked at Sammy. "Mark my words, by the time you get your first paycheck, Fred will announce who killed Henry." She turned back to me, opened her mouth to say something, and then her eyes widened. With a grin, she pointed over my shoulder. "I'm pretty sure *he's* not here for my baking." I followed her gaze and found Branson standing at the top of the steps, observing the packed space. From his expression, clearly Katie had been right.

"It was nice to meet you, Sammy. Sounds like we might be seeing a lot more of each other." I glared at Katie once more. "And you, don't go making things worse. There's enough gossip going around. I'm not getting involved."

She shrugged. "Whatever you say, Winifred Page."

After giving her a final glower, I turned, and Watson and I headed over to Branson. "Hey. Need some breakfast?"

He shook his head. "No, thank you. I'm here to talk to you, actually." He pointed down the steps. "Maybe we can go downstairs, have some privacy?"

"Of course."

He turned instantly and headed to the bookshop. I followed, Watson at my heels. I'd not caught even a glimmer of flirtation in Branson's eyes or in his tone. He had to be there for professional reasons.

As we got to the bottom of the steps, the front door opened, two women walked in, crossed the bookshop, gave a friendly nod in our direction, and headed up to the bakery. A glance around revealed that Branson and I were alone. "It's a good thing Katie opened the bakery upstairs. Otherwise all the books would be bored not getting to see anyone walk past them."

"I'm sure that will change. Your bookshop will do fine. At least once tourist season begins." Branson attempted a smile, but it didn't reach his eyes. For some reason, he seemed nervous again. He reached down to scratch Watson's head, but Watson ducked out of reach. "Not the cuddliest of dogs, is he?"

"No, never." It wasn't true. He went completely gaga over Barry—and Leo, for that matter. "I can tell you're not here to talk about Watson or the bookshop. What's going on?"

He didn't hesitate further, which I appreciated. "Obviously, I heard about what happened last night. We've been out at the murder scene all morning."

"And what? Has Officer Green determined that I was the one who killed him somehow?" I forced a laugh. Neither Branson nor Susan Green had been the officers to arrive at the park the night before, but Officer Green made no secret of hating my existence. Her doing such a thing wouldn't surprise me in the slightest, though I couldn't picture Branson going along with it.

"No, of course not. You're not involved this time. Not even as a witness. You've already given your statement as to what you saw, but you weren't even the first on the scene." Again, I had the impression he was nervous. "That's why I'm here, Fred, to let you know that, for once, you're not involved. None of your family is. None of your friends or anyone you're close to. I... didn't want you to worry."

"I know that. I wasn't worried. I was teasing about Susan, mostly." I started to laugh, but then I had a thought, one I knew with certainty was spot-on before I spoke. "But that's not why you're here, is it?" I tried to keep my voice neutral. "You're not concerned about me being worried. You're making it clear that I'm not involved, or more precisely, to keep my nose out of it."

He grimaced. "I didn't say that. Don't put words in my mouth. I would never word it like that to you."

Despite my efforts to keep my tone neutral, I placed my hands on my hips and narrowed my eyes. "So that isn't why you're here, then? You're okay with me putting my nose in it?"

He narrowed his eyes right back at me. "Why would you put your nose in it, Fred? It doesn't involve you."

Anger flitted through me, even though I'd been saying the exact same thing mere moments ago upstairs. "If I recall, the last time someone was killed in Estes, you gave your blessing for me to figure it out. And I did. Mostly."

"You were trying to clear your friend's name. I wasn't going to tell you no. But again, Henry's death has absolutely nothing to do with you. You need to stay out of it."

"I'm fairly certain I've made it clear that I don't like being told what to do." I knew it was ridiculous, and maybe even childish, but I tilted my chin and met him straight in the eyes, even if I did have to look up slightly to do it. "And I had absolutely no intention of getting involved."

He nodded, looking relieved momentarily, and then his green eyes narrowed once more. "*Had* no intention of getting involved?"

"Just what I said. I had no intention of getting involved." In the back of my mind, I could hear my mother chiding me for acting like a spoiled brat. But I could also hear my father laughing. "You're the one who came here, Sergeant Wexler. *You* came to *me*. I'd say you're the one trying to get me involved."

He rolled his eyes and crossed his arms over his chest. "Really? You're going to take that route? You're better than that, Fred."

"Am I? You think after a couple of dinners that you have me all figured out."

For a second he looked like he was going to argue, but then he shut his mouth and glared. Watson let out a soft warning grumbling in his throat, and Branson glanced down, then returned his attention to me. "You have skill, Fred, you do. And like I've told you before, you have your father's innate instincts." His tone had grown placating, but hardened again. "However, you own a bookshop. Stick to selling books for this case. Let the police do their job."

"I had no intention of...." My mind caught up with Branson's words. "What do you mean *this* case?" *Why this case? What's different about it?*

Once more I could swear Branson seemed flustered, but it was such a quick flash I couldn't truly be sure. "I already made that clear, Fred. *This* doesn't involve you. Your stepfather isn't accused of murder, neither is your friend and business partner. The only thing it has to do with you is that you happened to be in the same forest when Henry was killed. If somehow that makes you a suspect, then I suppose that would also be true for Katie... and Leo."

Watson whimpered at Leo's name.

Granted, Branson truly had hit one of my biggest triggers right on the head. After I left my marriage, I swore I would never be told what to do again, especially in a way thick with condescension, so maybe my haze of anger was coloring my perception. I was sure it was. Well, whatever. "Was that a threat? That if I don't listen to you then the police attention might turn toward Leo?"

"Don't be hysterical, Fred."

I laughed. It was that or punch him in the face. "Call me hysterical again, Branson, and I'll make sure to demonstrate to you what that word truly means."

"Now who's threatening?"

I opened my mouth to retort, but shut it again. He had a point. And even if he didn't, there was no good way for this to end if we kept going. As much as I hated to admit it, he was the policeman. I couldn't see him doing something as petty as arresting me or charging me with anything, but unlike him, a few dinners together didn't make me feel like I had the full measure of Branson Wexler. Which this conversation made more apparent. "Thank you for dropping by. I'm not sure if you noticed, but things are quite busy upstairs, and currently, Katie is the only paid person on staff dealing with the madness. I have work to do."

"Fred...." His voice softened, and he reached for me.

I took a step back.

Branson dropped his hand, but his voice lost all hardness. "I'm sorry. I really am. I know I handled this wrong."

For one disgusting moment, I nearly said it was okay, that I understood, and on the one hand, I did. He wasn't wrong. He was a policeman, a sergeant. *I* sold books. There was no other request he could make that would make any more sense, and I didn't care. "Yes. You did."

"Again, I'm sorry." He attempted a smile. "But even though I handled it poorly, I need to know that you understood."

"This is your way of fixing it? Implying that I don't understand simple English?" Okay, even I had to admit I was being petty at that point.

"Fred." His tone held a hint of warning.

"Yes, Sergeant Wexler. I heard your words, and I understood them. Thank you for checking."

He tilted his head, and I was certain he was about to ask me to clarify. That it wasn't enough to say that I understood, but that I would comply.

Maybe not an unreasonable request from a police officer to a civilian. But one that might prompt a second murder in this space in the span of a couple of months.

Seeming aware of that fact, he gave a sharp nod. "Very well. Glad we understand each other. And I am sorry that I've ended up offending you."

At least that much was different from my ex-husband. Although at this point, it wasn't nearly enough of a difference to matter. "I need to get back to Katie."

Another nod. "Have a good day, Fred." He glanced down. "You too, Watson."

I glared after him, watched him walk out the door and then out of sight past the large windows.

He was right. I knew that. And I was willing to bet Branson had done what my father would have if he'd been in a similar situation. Although I'd like to think my dad would've handled things smoother with a woman he cared about. And I truly did think Branson cared about me.

I also knew that in some way, I was being childish. I wasn't simply going to find out who killed Henry because Branson told me not to, but that was part of it. I couldn't pretend to care too much about Henry's death. It was horrible for anyone to be killed, but outside of getting to witness the body first-hand, it didn't feel any more personal than a story on the news. And, like Katie had implied, part of me had already been mapping out what might've happened. Maybe that would have been enough to get me involved. Probably so. But either way, Branson had made my choice perfectly clear.

I knelt and lowered my forehead to Watson's as I ruffled his flanks. "Want to go for a walk in the snow, buddy?"

I spent the rest of the day helping Katie in the bakery. By the time noon arrived, Sammy had on an apron and was officially employed by the Cozy Corgi bakery. And by closing, I'd managed to sell a whopping three books.

Leaving Katie to explain the ropes and her vision for the bakery to Sammy now that they weren't bombarded by customers, I loaded Watson into my burnt-orange Mini Cooper and drove to my little cabin in the woods. As we passed the new McMansion development, I wondered which house belonged to Silas. Even considered attempting to find out so I could see if he wanted to go along. He seemed calm and capable, and since he was an avid bird-watcher, was obviously observant. I knew it wasn't smart to go hiking in the woods alone, even if I had a dog. The other option was Leo, but there'd been enough romantic conflict for one day.

Within half an hour, I was bundled up in winter gear, having traded my broomstick skirt for snow pants. I attempted to put a scarf on Watson, but he wasn't having it.

I was relieved it wasn't Leo at the ranger station as we drove through and entered the national park. Within another twenty minutes, we arrived at the small parking lot at the beginning of the hikes that started with Bear Lake. Though it was a little after six, the sun was already gone and the sky nearly nighttime black, but it was brighter than the night before. Not a cloud to be seen, the moon full and glowing.

I checked to make sure I had a water bottle, my cell, and a flashlight. Then Watson and I took off.

Though not overly playful, every once in a while, Watson enjoyed being in the snow. I hadn't figured out the difference—half the time he acted like the white stuff was the biggest annoyance in the world, and the other half, like on this occasion, as if he was a five-year-old kid eating at Chuck E. Cheese's for the first time. Not even minding being on a leash, Watson buried his nose in the thicker piles of snow by the trail and bulldozed through as we walked, reminding me of the old Disney cartoons of chipmunks burrowing under the ground and leaving a trail behind them.

I hadn't been sure I'd be able to find the location where Henry was killed, but that part turned out to be easy. Maybe I should've expected it. There hadn't been fresh snowfall that day, and while many trails and footpaths crisscrossed all around Bear Lake, it was clear where the most traveled path was. It had been walked over so much in the hours since the murder that most of the snow was gone, revealing the dirt and rock beneath.

No police tape marked the scene. I had been prepared to walk right past it, mentally sticking my tongue out at Branson as I did so, but it seemed the police had gathered everything they needed. Surely they'd searched the entire area. So not only was I being childish, I was also being ridiculous, thinking I'd find anything they hadn't.

The spot where Henry's body had lain was mostly clear, with patches of snow here and there, and a small amount of bloodstain still visible.

For a second, I considered releasing Watson from his leash and giving him free rein to use his powerful dog nose to find things I couldn't see. But Leo had warned me when I first met him that it wasn't uncommon for mountain lions and coyotes to snatch family pets right out of the yard, even with people nearby. I might want to prove that Branson couldn't tell me what to do, but not at the cost of risking Watson.

We traipsed over the area for probably half an hour, Watson clearly most interested in the site of the killing. All the smells. But neither of us uncovered anything other than displaced rocks and broken twigs in the underbrush.

By the time a quarter after seven rolled around, I was freezing. It seemed colder than the night before, but maybe that was simply because I wasn't distracted. I was about to give up, when I remembered Leo's directions to Katie and me from the night before. I leaned against a large barren aspen and closed my eyes, letting the stillness of the evening blanket me. Like before, for a few minutes I heard nothing, and then it changed, slowly. Again, the wind was the first thing I noticed, with the rustle of branches overhead. Then Watson's breathing and his quiet footfalls as he padded around me. After a few more heartbeats, I heard scampering through the twigs and scraggly plants near our feet.

Then a quiet chirp.

I opened my eyes. At first I didn't see him, but

then he moved. A mountain jay, its shiny black head glistening in the moonlight as it pecked at the ground where Henry had been killed. I didn't let myself think about what he might be pecking at.

Maybe he sensed my attention, because he looked over in my direction and tilted his head. He then hopped a few feet farther away. Though jays were almost as common as pigeons in the city, I paused at his beauty, the rich blue of his feathers visible even in the dim light. He hopped several more yards, still inspecting Watson and me every couple of leaps, and then came to rest a short distance from where Henry had been killed. He began to peck the ground below another tree. He pecked again, and something glinted in the moonlight at his feet. Another chirp, another peck, and then Watson rushed toward him, moving so fast his leash slid off my wrist and dragged after him through the snow.

"Watson!"

He didn't listen, and the bird flew away before Watson was even halfway to it.

Watson stopped where the bird had been pecking, and I finished my rush to him and snatched up his leash. "What in the world are you doing? Trying to get eaten? Since when do you chase birds? Or play, for that matter?"

Watson gave me an unapologetic glance and then sat down in the snow with a huff.

A chirp from above made me glance up, and I found the jay looking down at us from a branch overhead. He was clearly mocking, though whether his judgment was aimed at me or Watson wasn't so obvious.

Remembering the flash I'd noticed as the jay had been pecking away at something, I searched the ground. I found several rocks, limitless pinecones, and just as many broken twigs and branches. Then, half-buried in snow, it caught the moonlight.

Slipping off my glove, I reached down and picked up the cold metal, then wiped the snow off against my jacket before lifting it to the light.

A silver pin. Similar to the one Katie now owned. It was a strangely-shaped bird with glistening greenish brown stones acting as feathers. I had no idea what type of bird it was, not that it mattered. I didn't need to know the bird. I already knew *whose* it was, which was much more important. Though I didn't think I'd seen this exact pin on her, it matched the style of ones Myrtle wore.

Watson whimpered in anticipation as I knocked on the apartment door. He sniffed all around the base and looked up at me in excitement. That made one of us. I was torn between feeling nervous and wondering if I was being stupid.

Leo opened the door and cut off my concerns. Actually, Watson's frantic barking was probably what cut off my thoughts. Leo attempted to say hello to me, but wisely lavished his attention where needed most by dropping to both knees and giving Watson the belly rub of his life.

"You're going to find corgi hair in the most random places in your apartment for weeks now." I stepped past the two of them into the warmth. "Welcome to my life."

Leo grinned up at me, looking nearly as happy as Watson. "Small price to pay for getting love lavished like this."

That was true. I wasn't one of those who thought because a dog liked someone it meant they were a good person, or that dogs innately knew if people were evil. I'd be willing to bet Watson would forgive an intruder two minutes after murdering me if they had a big enough dog treat. But on the whole, I figured it was a good sign when my little grump was accepting of someone.

To my surprise, when Leo stood, shut the door, and led us into his apartment, Watson reclaimed his spot by my side, managing to pad along without tripping me. Though he kept his adoring gaze on Leo.

"Welcome to my home. It's not much, but better than some." He motioned toward the kitchen. "Would you like a drink? I'm not a big alcohol kinda guy, but I have water.... And maybe some pink-lemonade mix."

"Pink-lemonade mix?" I couldn't help but laugh. "I don't think I've gotten an offer for that since I was ten."

He shrugged. "It's pretty good. Nothing but sugar, but it brings back good memories."

Talk about a different experience from the three-hundred-dollar bottle of wine Branson had ordered for our first meal together. Chances were high my class level put me at more of a pink lemonade kind of gal. "I'm okay, thanks, but if you don't mind a bowl of water for Watson?"

"Of course. Be right back."

As Leo headed to the kitchen, I took the time to inspect his apartment. I wasn't sure if it was because Leo was younger or just a stereotypical man. The space was clean... spotless, but there wasn't much to it. The furniture seemed more for complete convenience than any aesthetic design. There were some pictures scattered here and there of people I assumed were family, but little else to make the place feel homey.

Leo was back in less than a minute, set a bowl at Watson's feet, and then motioned toward the couch. "Want to fill me in? You sounded a little flustered."

I sat on the edge of the couch closest to Watson, and Leo took the other side, leaving an empty cushion between us. I decided not to clarify the "flustered" comment. Better let him think my discovery on the moonlight hike had affected me. In truth, I'd been torn about calling Branson to show him the pin, but figured it would end in another argument. Leo seemed a more natural option, though for some odd reason, part of me felt guilty for dragging him into it.

I opted to cut to the chase and pulled the pin out of my pocket. "Watson and I did a little snooping around where Henry was killed last night. We found this."

Leo lifted the pin from my hand, his honey-brown eyes going wide. "Myrtle's."

"Yeah. That's what I thought too. I don't know if I've seen her wear this exact one, but it's definitely her style."

"You know, I can't say that I have either. But she

has a ton of them." He inspected it again. "It's a kakapo. Native to New Zealand and critically endangered."

"Well, that definitely sounds like a bird Myrtle would care about."

Leo gave a halfhearted shrug. "I don't think there's a bird in existence that Myrtle doesn't care about." He chuckled softly. "She's nearly as concerned about those already extinct as she is the ones we have now." He twisted the jewelry, a sad expression crossing his face. "You found this where Henry was killed?"

I nodded. "A few yards away, but basically, yes." For some reason, the next thought hadn't entered my mind until that very moment. I wasn't sure how I missed it before. "A mountain jay found it for us. Seems fitting for Myrtle, doesn't it?"

He chuckled again. "That it does. Although if you are thinking what I think you're thinking, it would be kind of sad that a bird, of all things, would be Myrtle's undoing."

I wasn't sure what I was thinking anymore. So many possibilities had flitted through my mind on the drive over that I couldn't land on one in particular that seemed to make sense. "You know, when I picked it up, that's where I went instantly. That

Myrtle must've been the killer, or at least been there when Henry was murdered. But the pin wasn't the murder weapon, and it wasn't right where he lay either. By the time the police got there, the entire Feathered Friends Brigade had all stomped around that area. It could have easily fallen off her coat."

That realization had bothered me the night before as well, once I got home. I was a policeman's daughter. The least I could've done was a better job at securing the scene. Of course, I also realized on my way over to Leo that I'd messed up again. I'd picked up the pin with my bare fingers and removed it from the scene. Though, in my defense, it had already been cleared and was no longer a crime scene. Either way, my prints were all over it, as were Leo's now.

"I take it you're investigating Henry's murder?"

I paused for a second, trying to determine if I'd heard judgment in Leo's tone. I didn't think so. "I don't know, honestly. I don't have a reason to. No one I know very well or care about is under suspicion. I'm probably being stupid." I couldn't bring myself to admit to Leo that at least some part of it was simply due to Branson telling me that I couldn't. Though, that honestly wasn't the largest part.

An expression crossed Leo's face that I couldn't name. Not nervous, but... something.... Finally he licked his lips and narrowed his eyes. "I know you and Branson are close. So please don't take this as a slight against him, but I haven't had the best experience with the police department in this town." He winced. "Maybe that's not fair to single him out. I've had a few interactions with him, to be sure, that haven't gone well, but the same is true for many of the other officers. It's not just Branson. Every concern I've had about poaching was dismissed. You finding the owl was the first breakthrough we've had. And I know the members of the bird club have had similar experiences."

"Well, yes, but you can't blame Branson for that. I've attended two functions with them—including the blowup at the opening night of the bookshop, three—and every single one involved accusations against its own members. Granted, those were all from Henry, but it's hard to take it seriously."

It was easy to see the walls beginning to form behind Leo's eyes.

I rushed ahead to try to stop the damage I'd accidentally done, and in so doing reached out and touched his thigh briefly without meaning to. "I didn't say that to defend Branson. We had a disagreement about all of this. And I've seen enough to know that even if the Feathered Friends

Brigade brought the entire case solved on a platter that there's so much bad history between the bird club and the police department, they probably wouldn't even give it a second thought." A twinge of guilt bit at me for betraying Branson, which was ridiculous. I wasn't betraying him, nor did I owe him anything.

The walls crumbled just that easily. "Yeah. Exactly." Leo laughed again, the ease truly back. "Don't get me wrong, I can't entirely blame Branson or the police. There's a limited number of times you can experience the cry-wolf effect before you quit listening. Even me—Henry was trying to tell me his thoughts on the poaching that very night. I didn't listen. Not that it means he was right this time. But when you accuse everyone under the sun, at some point, maybe you finally land on the right person."

I sat up a little straighter. I'd not thought of it like that. "So you're thinking maybe he truly did know the poacher this time, and that person killed him."

"Maybe. Though I can't see the poacher in that group. Most of them genuinely have a strong passion about birds. There's a couple, like Paulie, who I think are just there for the social aspect, but that's rare."

Excitement buzzed through me, and if there'd been any question whether I was going to continue, that faded away. "Who was the last person Henry accused? Owen, right?"

He scrunched up his nose as he thought. "Yes, I believe so. Two days before had been Roxanne, and last week he was accusing Myrtle again." He held up the kakapo pin once more, as if seeing Myrtle's face on it. "The two of them had a strained relationship. Or at least Henry had a strange relationship with her. One minute she was nearly like a savior to him who deserved worship, and the next she was a traitor who was using the club for her own gain in power."

"What do you think?"

He came back to the moment and grinned at me, his fondness clear. "Interviewing witnesses, Detective Page?"

"Oh, sorry. I didn't mean to treat you like that."

Leo laughed and shook his head. "I'm teasing. Well, kinda. It's a good look on you." At that moment, Watson leapt from the floor onto the cushion between us.

"Watson! Get down. You're not at home."

Though he glowered at me, he started to oblige, but Leo placed his hand on Watson's head.

"As long as he's not breaking rules from your house, it's fine with me. I kinda love the little guy.

Although, how could I not? I rarely get such rock-star treatment. Basically it's just Watson and my mom."

My heart warmed suddenly, though I couldn't quite say why. I focused on Watson instead. "Fine. Enjoy the couch. Try not to completely cover the cushions in your fur."

In way of response, Watson rolled over on his back, accepted belly scratches from both of us, and made a Watson-size cloud of hair billow around the three of us.

Leo grinned over at me. "He's not exactly subtle, is he?"

"You have no idea." I offered a grimace. "Maybe he gets that from me. So, I believe you were getting ready to tell me your thoughts about Myrtle?"

He laughed again, and I realized I was getting used to that sound. "She's a trip, to be sure. And I wouldn't completely disagree with Henry. She likes her power and being in control, but I honestly don't think it's about her. She's obsessed with birds, but not owning them or collecting them like so many. She wants to save them." He started rubbing Watson's paws. I was pretty sure the earth had stopped moving—Watson didn't let anyone do that. "But if I'm being honest, I have to fully admit I have a blind spot where Myrtle's concerned. It's rare for people to feel as passionate about animals as I do, or in Myrtle's case, even more so. At times it can feel like there's a handful of you trying to make a difference. And she is. She's trying to make a difference. So I can't see her in a bad light. The only reason I could ever picture her killing somebody was if she found out they were poaching her birds."

I sucked in a breath, and Leo looked over at me. "Maybe that's it exactly. Maybe Henry was the one poaching and he spent all his time accusing everyone else. What's that saying? The lady doth protest too much? He wouldn't be the first one to try such a thing."

Leo shrugged. "Maybe. Although he was pretty passionate about birds as well. Perhaps he's the kind who liked to collect them? I can't say. In a lot of ways, he was as crazy as Myrtle about it all. But there is something with Myrtle that lets you connect. Whatever that thing is, it was missing with Henry."

Both our gazes traveled to the pin on the sofa by Watson.

Leo picked it up once more. "You going to take this to Branson?"

"I suppose I have to. Although I don't know how he's going to handle it. He made it very clear to keep my nose out of it this time."

Leo considered for a moment. "I can take it. Say that I found it when I went back to the scene. In fact you can take me there now and show me exactly where you found it so I can show him. That way you're not in danger of being shut out of the case or getting in trouble."

And look at that—he brought up one of the very options I'd been considering on the way over. Words I hadn't been sure how to bring myself to ask. Now I didn't have to. He offered it up like the easiest thing in the world.

And as the words left his lips, I knew my answer. I prided myself on being Charles Page's daughter. No child of his would lie about a murder investigation. "No. But thank you. That's something I'll have to do myself. I can handle him."

And once more Leo's lovely laugh filled the space between us. "Oh, Fred, I have no doubt of that. I can't imagine anyone you can't handle."

SEVEN

The last time Watson and I had entered the police station, we were running for our lives. Technically, I was running and Watson was in my arms, a position he detests. One might think once a location became a safe haven there was no way it could ever be anything other. But nothing about walking through the front doors of the police station this time came close to feeling like relief.

After my last conversation with Branson, I could already feel my temperature rising. I wasn't breaking any laws, wasn't impeding an investigation, and it wasn't my fault that I'd done a better job of detective work than the entire police department since I'd moved to Estes. And I was done being told what to do.

After I held open the door for Watson and glanced toward the front desk, another surprise flitted through me. Officer Green was talking to the policeman at the desk, who I believed was the same gentleman Watson and I had burst in on the last time we were there. And upon seeing her, a twisted miracle happened. I was glad it was Officer Green and not Branson. I never would've dreamed of that happening in a million years.

As always, when Susan Green looked at me and sneered at Watson, I could swear I heard Miss Gulch promising threats, followed by, *and your little dog too....*

"Hello. Good to see you, Officer Green." I nodded toward the other policeman but didn't attempt to recall his name.

Susan flinched, confusion washing over her features. Neither of us had ever said it was good to see the other. From our first meeting on, there'd been nothing but hostility. And while I considered her the bigger perpetrator, it went both ways.

"Winifred. It's good to...." Clearly unable to say the words, she turned her solid bulk to look at me full-on. "Are you needing police assistance?"

This was going better than normal as well. I pulled the pin from my pocket and started to close the distance to the counter but was jerked up short by Watson's leash. Looking back, apparently some snow had fallen off his fur and he was having a little snack on the go. I gave a pleading yank to his leash, and he huffed, clearly affronted, then with narrowed eyes took a final lick of the melting treat and uncharacteristically followed directions.

Officer Green's sneer was more pronounced as I turned back. Her pale blue eyes clearly revealing that she would spit-roast a corgi if she got the chance.

Okay, maybe this wasn't going better than normal.

"Watson and I found this on our—" I cleared my throat. "—moonlight walk through the national park. I thought maybe this could be important evidence."

Susan didn't reach for the pin—simply studied it for a second, glared at me, then repeated the pattern several times. After a moment, Officer What's His Name stretched out his hand for it, only to have Susan grip his wrist and shove his hand away.

I should have been upfront. Although in my defense, there was no way I could've played this out that would've ended pleasantly.

"Moonlight walk through the national park, huh?" She finally took the jewelry, studied it for less than a heartbeat, and then gave me the cold ice of her stare once more. "You know, Miss Page, normal people don't traipse back through the woods alone in the dark, even with their guard dog that's more the size of a fat hamster, and parade through a crime scene that's less than a day old." She smiled, sort of. Whatever it was, it wasn't a smile at all. "Of course, I should've stopped when I said *normal* people."

I cleared my throat again, and to my surprise once more, I decided that I preferred this interaction to anything I would've had with Branson. Susan and I weren't exactly cordial to each other, but neither of us were expected to be. "You've got me there, Susan. One thing I've never claimed was being normal. And this wasn't exactly at the crime scene; it was several yards away. And... there was no tape."

"Right." She looked like she was enjoying herself finally. "Because you don't see walking through yellow police tape like somehow crossing a finish line."

I started to object, but the description was apt. One I wouldn't have thought of, but she was spot-on. Especially this time, with my desire to solve it before Branson or anyone else.

Officer Green held the pin up between us. "You know, Fred, while not overly impressed with your attempts to play Nancy Drew, at least with the evidence you found at Christmas, you had the sense to put it in a Ziploc bag. How much show-and-tell did you do on this little ditty before you brought it to me? Should I expect to find half of the town's finger-prints on it?"

I nearly pointed out that I most definitely did not bring it to *her*, but I reminded myself that I was a thirty-eight-year-old woman, and there was no reason to return to schoolyard cattiness. "I'll agree with you there. I wasn't thinking clearly when I picked the pin out of the snow."

She leaned forward, barely enough to be deci-pherable, but I could feel the hunger in the action. "Goodness. That's embarrassing. Wasn't your daddy a police officer?"

It didn't matter that we were in a police station, nor that she would happily throw Watson and me into separate cells in the back. Susan had hit a nerve, and she was about to see the unleashed fury that all redheads share, no matter what the shade, when Ser-geant Wexler appeared as if by magic from the hallway beside the counter.

"Fred. I thought I heard your voice." Branson smiled at me like our last interaction hadn't been tense in the slightest. He even went so far as to walk around the counter, squeeze my arm gently, and pat Watson, who allowed it to happen for about two whole seconds. Then he refocused on me, his handsome face easy and approachable. "What brings you in?"

Officer Green didn't give me the chance to respond. Leaning over the counter, she thrust the pin between us. "Our local busybody bookshop owner brought us the evidence we need to crack the case of who killed crazy man Henry. And due to her considerate nature, she didn't want us to spend police resources fingerprinting the thing, so she passed it around town."

Though Branson winced at Susan's tone, his green eyes cooled, then hardened. Despite myself, I straightened a little under the weight of his glare. "I thought I made myself clear, Fred. You said you understood."

His voice was low but not low enough that Susan and the other officer wouldn't be able to hear. For his part, the officer who was nameless had the grace to look uncomfortable. Susan appeared to be experiencing Christmas for a second time a few weeks later.

Well, if Branson wasn't going to have this conversation in private, I wasn't about to cower. I straightened to my full height. "You're right. I did say I understood, but I didn't agree to anything. And if we're pointing fingers...." I demonstrated by pointing my finger at the pin still in Susan's hand. "It's a good thing I did. As your department had already scoured the area and seemed to overlook something."

He didn't so much as miss a beat, not even to look at the pin. "So please tell me how to do my job, Fred. What would you like me to do? Doubtless you've deduced that the pin is more than likely Myrtle Bantam's. Do I take it to her and ask if she shoved it into Henry's throat before the knife? Do I assume it's hers because, out of all the people the officers found traipsing around the dead body when they arrived, she is Henry's killer? Or perhaps only the killer would be fool enough to drop some perfectly placed clue for you to stumble upon?"

"My guess is that her dog found it. Isn't he the real detective? After all, he found the candy that cracked the case when Opal was killed." Christmas had indeed come for Susan Green. I knew there wasn't any love lost between her and Branson, but clearly she couldn't help herself. "And it was him that got a craving for pizza which led to the most heart-stopping car chase through town that's ever happened with people who weren't on mopeds."

Branson flashed her a look, one that said to be silent, but that was all. He turned back to me and folded his arms. "Well? You obviously don't respect what we do here, nor me requesting nicely for you to let me do my job. So you might as well tell me what to do next."

Once more, my indignation flared. I decided to leave with as much dignity as I could muster. "I've never told you how to do your job, Sergeant Wexler. And if I thought you weren't able to do it, I wouldn't have brought you the pin, which was apparently overlooked at the site. What you do next is up to you." I turned to leave, hoping Watson wouldn't stop at the puddle that was between us and the door.

"No more moonlight strolls, Miss Page. Otherwise it might be considered police interference."

I didn't look back at Susan. I knew if I did, I genuinely would lose my temper. "Last I checked, the national park belongs to all people, *Miss* Green."

Thankfully Watson decided the puddle was beneath him. Not only wasn't he tempted to eat it, but decided he was too good to walk through it. He took the wide way around, and then we walked proudly out the front door.

Things weren't quite as hectic at the Cozy Corgi the

next morning. Even so, there was a decent rush for coffee and pastries, but it seemed more people simply wanted breakfast than gossip about the latest murder. I didn't even get to talk to Katie very much, no more than to fill her in on the previous night's events. She was still busy between customers and training Sammy.

Strangely, I was a little sad about Sammy. Obviously Katie and I both needed help, but it had been nice adjusting to our store with only the two of us. Although, even upon the second meeting, I was blown away that Katie had somehow managed to find her doppelgänger. It was uncanny.

That was a quality I most definitely was not going to look for when I decided to hire someone for the bookshop.

It had been at least an hour since I sold a book, or since anyone had done more than wave as they made the trek from the front door to the stairs leading to the bakery. I studied Watson as he slept in the rays of the sun pouring through the large windows. He'd claimed a spot closer to the front door than I would've predicted, now that we had people coming and going. He was surrounded by books and looked so charming there, his orange fur shiny, the hardwood floor gleaming, with the backdrop of rows and rows of novels.

That was one more reminder of why I was in town. Not to get my heart dashed by Branson Wexler, *which was not happening*, nor to have it comforted by Leo Lopez, *which was not happening either*. I was here for the Cozy Corgi and to enjoy life.

Well, I was going to do just that—even if I did have to keep reminding myself.

I wandered into the mystery room, picked up a reprint of Agatha Christie's *A Body in the Library*, and plopped myself down on the sofa in front of the fire. From where I sat, I could look over my shoulder and see Watson napping away, could still hear his soft snores.

Yes, this was why I was here. And with the soft sounds of chatter, clink of dishes, and hum of machines joining the heavenly aroma wafting from above, it was even better than I'd pictured.

I barely made it three chapters in before Katie appeared in the doorway. "Fred! There you are."

I shut the book and started to stand, but she motioned for me to stay where I was, then plopped down beside me.

She sighed and dragged her fingers through her

hair, leaving trails of flour or icing behind. "I needed a break, and I wanted to tell you the gossip." She glanced around the base of the sofa. "Where's Watson?" Without waiting for a reply, she glanced over her shoulder and chuckled. "Working hard, I see."

At that moment Watson let out a quiet little bark and his paws twitched.

"I'm pretty sure he's either dreaming about especially large dog treats when he does that or possibly dreaming about another nap."

"Sounds about right." She turned back to me. "I might be tired, but even this, simply being able to walk downstairs and talk to you for two minutes is an improvement. Sammy is going to be worth her weight in gold."

"I'm sure I should follow your lead and start looking for someone to help me out in the bookstore, not that it's been an issue today." I shook my head at the thought of an assistant without a single thing to do. I'd have to find someone who didn't like mysteries so they could read in a different room and leave me to my sofa, lamp, and fireplace in peace. "Perhaps I should worry about selling books before I hire someone."

Katie patted my knee. "Don't feel bad. Books are

a different thing than pastries. People need sugar every day. But when they need a book, they'll come here." She leaned closer to play-whisper, "Well, forget about Amazon for the moment." She winked. "At least when the tourist season arrives, you'll be busy."

I wasn't going to admit that I wasn't overly worried about it. Simply sitting here by the fire reading was about as perfect as things could get. "So what's the gossip?"

Katie's brown eyes widened. "Well, Benjamin was upstairs. He's the one who owns the camera shop down the way. He's a member of the Feathered Friends Brigade, remember?"

"Yeah, the handsome young one who seemed like he was making a sales pitch."

She nodded. "Exactly. I kinda think that's why he's there. He's tenacious, I'll give him that. He tried a sales pitch on me and Sammy, saying that we needed a high-quality camera so we could post photos of all the pastries online, to bring in more customers." She gave a dismissive wave with her hand. "Like I have time for that. And that wasn't my point." Before launching in again, she glanced around to see if anyone had wandered near as we spoke, a laughable thought considering no one was in the bookshop. "Well, according to Benjamin, the police brought Myrtle in for questioning this morning. I'm still not clear on how he found out about it so quickly, but he said he drove straight there and told them that she was with him at the exact same moment Henry was killed." She narrowed her eyes. "Which I suppose could be true. Honestly, I lost track of time when you, Leo, and I were watching the elk, but the last I'd seen of Myrtle, she was with Silas, not Benjamin. Though, I don't remember seeing Benjamin much at all. I mean, obviously he was there, but I never saw him around Myrtle."

I wished I'd been upstairs devouring another pastry I didn't need instead of reading by the fire so I could have judged Benjamin for myself. "You got the impression he was lying?"

She shrugged. "No, not necessarily. It doesn't match what I remember, but again, there's nothing for me to remember—we split up, and then the three of us saw some elk." Another shrug. "Plus, not that I know Myrtle, obviously, but I can't see her and Benjamin chatting it up. You know what I mean? I don't think he's a true bird lover like the rest. I kinda think he's there to sell camera equipment more than anything about birds."

"I had a similar thought, actually, but at the tune

of ten thousand a year, is that intelligent advertising?" Camera equipment was expensive, so maybe he only needed a few sales a year to make it up. "What'd he say about Myrtle? Did he know how the police questioning ended up?"

"That's what I'm getting at. Benjamin said as soon as he heard about them taking Myrtle in, that he drove straight there and let them know that they were together."

"So with him as her alibi, they couldn't hold her. Especially if all they had on her was the pin I told you about earlier."

"Exactly." She cocked an eyebrow and gave an excited grin. "So, I was thinking you and I should leave Sammy here, and we can go up to Wings of the Rockies and get Myrtle's version."

"You're determined that I'm going to play detective on this, aren't you?"

Katie rolled her eyes. "No more than you are, and don't tell me otherwise. I know you and I haven't known each other all that long, but there's one thing I'm certain about—Winifred Page doesn't let a man tell her what she can or cannot do, even if that man happens to wear a badge."

As so often was the case in my conversations with Katie, I was reminded of one of the many reasons I loved her so. "I'm sure I shouldn't admit it, but you're right. I can't say I'm certain my father would approve of going against another officer's wishes, but I'm not letting this go." At the thought, I started to stand to head straight to Myrtle, but then logic took over and I sat back down. "However, if you'll remember, it was Myrtle Bantam who called and complained about me when I was trying to clear Barry's name. Basically told Branson I was harassing the storeowners. I can't imagine a conversation with her going well right now, especially if she knows I'm the one that turned in the pin. And while I don't think Branson would tell her that, if she came in contact with Susan Green, I guarantee you that would get passed on."

Katie let out a little growl. "Dang it! I suppose that makes sense, but I really wanted to go talk to her."

Now *there* was a thought. I sat up straighter, excitement flooding back. "That's a brilliant idea. She loves you. If you had ten grand, you'd be in her club right now. I bet you anything she'll talk to you."

Katie looked nervous. "Without you? You want me to go? Without you?"

This time I was the one who squeezed her knee. "Don't be silly. We both know all you need to do to get her talking is to spend five minutes on Google looking up facts about that kakapo bird and chances are you won't leave her store until closing."

"Brilliant!" She pulled out her cell and began typing away. I was certain she would be an encyclopedia about the endangered species within half an hour. "What will you do while I'm talking to Myrtle?"

No use pretending I wasn't going to play detective again. "I think I'll wake Watson and go to gossip headquarters. Luckily, I don't have to do any research to get Anna and Carl talking. And for once, with him being part of the club, it'll be some first-hand knowledge."

EIGHT

Watson seemed to forgive me for disrupting his nap when he realized we were walking toward Cabin and Hearth. He'd come to equate the store with his favorite dog treats instead of the home furnishings and high-end log furniture it sold. Apparently it didn't matter that Katie was now making those treats in large quantities right above our heads. Watson went from sulking and sluggish at the end of his leash to bouncing on his front paws as we walked through the shop's doors.

If I'd been feeling guilty about ignoring the police edict to leave well enough alone, or wondering if I was disappointing my father as he looked down on me, all such notions fled when I approached the front counter of Cabin and Hearth.

Not only were Anna and Carl present and accounted for, but they were flanked by my uncles.

With so much natural talent for gossip gathered in one place, the home furnishing store might've been a front for a new tabloid publication. It was like the universe was flashing the green light saying, "Here you go, Fred, figure it out. Solve that murder, and show that handsome police officer that he can't tell you what to do, even if it is his job." Okay, maybe that wasn't exactly the message, but I was going to take it that way, regardless.

I nearly laughed as the four of them turned as one to look at Watson and me. Then for a second, it didn't so much seem like a miracle provided from the gossip gods as much as stumbling into a nest of hungry vampires. The look in their eyes was ravenous. So much so that I took a step back. Watson whined, but I wasn't sure if he felt the same intensity in their stare or if he was begging for a snack.

"Hi, guys." I managed a wave. "What are you all up to?"

"Talking about you, naturally." Blunt as always, Percival left the group, grabbed my hand, and ushered me to join the others.

Anna and Carl were on the other side of the counter, and I took my place between Gary and Percival, closing the circle. Watson nudged his head against the back of my calf. I ignored him.

Anna reached across the counter and grasped my hand. "Perfect timing, dear. We were going to come find you in a few minutes. Fill us in."

"Fill you in on what?" Even as the words left my mouth, I wasn't sure why I bothered.

Percival rolled his eyes, but Anna used her other hand to pat mine. "None of that. You're the one who took Myrtle's pin to the police last night, and then she was brought in for questioning this morning. So, fill us in."

"How do you all do that? Did you install surveillance cameras in the police department?" I narrowed my eyes at Gary. Though he could hold his own, he was the least natural gossip of the four. "I'm sure Branson didn't tell you, and I know Officer Green hates you and Percival nearly as much as she does me, since you're part of the family." I turned to Anna and Carl. "Is she your in? Do you two have a special relationship with Susan that I'm not aware of?"

"We never reveal our sources, dear." Anna released my hand and patted her poufy cloud of white hair while managing to look dead serious. "And you came to us, remember? Don't pretend you're not here hoping to finagle some details from us."

Percival snickered. "You can act like you don't want the gossip, Fred. But you come by it naturally. It's in the Oswald blood, even if your mother isn't especially good at it. Maybe it skips generations or something. And while it took a different form, your father was good at it too. It's what made him such a great detective." He nudged my shoulder with his. "So give in, favorite niece of mine, and dish."

I did. Filling them in on Watson's and my moonlit hike, finding the pin, my interactions at the police station, and what Benjamin told Katie.

Percival threw his long arm over my shoulder and squeezed. "Oh, darling, I'm so sorry that there's already trouble in paradise between you and that handsome sergeant. Don't give up hope. We can rope him into being part of the family yet."

Gary patted my arm comfortingly but leveled his dark gaze at his husband. "I don't think that was the point of the story, Percival." He gave me a wincing smile. "But I am sorry about that, too."

Carl ignored them. "Benjamin told the police he was with Myrtle when Henry was killed?" For once, his words weren't laced with the enjoyment of a scandal, but sounded more like actual confusion. "That's odd."

All eyes turned toward Carl.

He straightened at the attention, seeming pleased. "Well, that isn't quite how I remember it that evening."

"She couldn't quite explain why, but Katie didn't completely buy Benjamin's story. Something seemed off." I knew I'd come to the right place. "What do you remember from that night?"

Settling into the role of center of attention, Carl leaned against the counter and propped his weight on his elbows. "Well, in full disclosure, I was a bit distracted that evening. Ever since Paulie joined the Feathered Friends Brigade, he's seemed insistent that he and I become BFFs. So I spent a good chunk of the night avoiding him, which is rather like a full-time job. But I teamed up with Roxanne, who has the most badges for her trivia knowledge about birds. After a few minutes, we ran into Raul and Lucy."

Anna interrupted by reaching across the counter once more and touching my arm. "You know Raul, don't you, Fred? He owns Pasta Thyme. Where you and Branson went on your first date? I heard you had a very good bottle of wine."

"What?" Percival went ultrasonic, eliciting a sharp whimper from Watson. He wheeled toward me. "You didn't tell me that? You made it sound like you simply grabbed a meal a couple of times. You didn't say it was at Pasta Thyme or that there was wine involved." He snapped a hand on his jutted hip. "That isn't a meal. That is a *date*. I had no idea things were moving so expediently." He waggled excited eyebrows at Gary. "Can you imagine the gorgeous great nephews and great nieces those two will give us." Before Gary or anyone else could respond, Percival's expression crashed into disappointment, and he looked back at me. "Oh, I forgot. You two are already having problems. We need to figure that out."

I couldn't even think of how to respond to any of that, and I looked to Gary for help. He simply shrugged. "What do you expect, Fred? You have met your uncle before."

He had a point. I refocused on Carl. "You said that you teamed up with Roxanne and the two of you bumped into Raul and Lucy. Right?" Maybe we could get the show back on the road.

He nodded emphatically. "Yes, exactly. I do think Raul genuinely cares about birds, even if he doesn't have any badges, and he's very committed to the cause. But Lucy...." He waffled his hand back and forth. "I'm pretty sure she's there for discounted bird feed from Myrtle's store."

"Discounted bird feed?" I gaped at him. "She's

paying ten grand a year to be in a club for discounted bird feed?"

"Well"—Carl shrugged—"a discount is a discount."

All four of the older generation nodded, and I realized I had gotten pulled off track, again. I shook my head, trying to clear it, only to have Percival gasp and reach toward my ears.

"Are these the earrings Leo Lopez gave you at the grand opening?" He twisted the dangling chain of corgis, causing me to adjust the angle of my head to keep it from pinching. "They are! Well, you truly are a niece of mine. I couldn't be prouder. Romancing *two* handsome men." He reached behind my back and swatted at Gary. "Our great nieces and great nephews might be of the Hispanic persuasion. We'll be so cutting-edge."

Gary cocked a judgmental eyebrow, then cast me a withering glance. "He said the same thing to me at our proposal. If we hadn't been together for over twenty years, I'd have been fairly certain he was with me because I was black, not actually because he loved me."

Percival's expression changed once more, and he turned wide eyes on me again. "Oh no, I just thought! You're thirty-eight, Fred. Better get moving."

I sighed, not sure if I should laugh or cry. "Goodness, the four of you together are a lot to handle. If we could try to stay on track, and not worry about the ticking away of my childbearing years, and get back to the case. Besides, I have Watson. If you have a corgi, who needs a kid?"

"Watson!" It was Anna's turn to suck in a gasp as she threw her hands in the air, as she was prone to do. "Oh my heavens, I was so caught up in the excitement I didn't even notice my favorite little man." She ran from behind the counter and smacked Carl's arm, another thing she was inclined to do. "Go get him one of the treats. Quick."

Knowing there was no reason to protest, I settled back and watched the fiasco. Anna rushed from behind the counter, all heaving bosom and gingham material billowing around Watson a she threw herself at him while Carl lumbered to the back to retrieve the treat.

Percival and Gary had never seen Anna with Watson before, as they kept casting wide-eyed stares over my head at each new promise of devotion and declaration of adoration that Anna lavished on my corgi.

Finally Carl returned, and knowing his role, handed the large all-natural dog treat to Anna so she could, in turn, present it as an offering to Watson.

And Watson, as *he* was prone to do, once receiving his treat, rejected further physical adoration and waddled to a large four-poster log bed, squeezed underneath, and relished his treasure.

Anna watched him contentedly for a few seconds and then returned to her place behind the counter. "So, Fred, quit dillydallying and fill us in."

I managed a smile before looking back at Carl. "I believe it was you who was filling us in. What did you see about Benjamin that made you think he wasn't with Myrtle?"

"Oh yes! I almost forgot." I couldn't say I blamed him for that. He nodded, licked his lips, and then launched in once more. "So, like I was saying, Roxanne and I were looking for the Mexican Spotted Owl and ran into Raul and Lucy." To my surprise, there was no further commentary about the new players. "I was a little annoyed they wanted to join us—it makes it a lot less likely to find the bird you're looking for with more people traipsing around—but I think Roxanne has a secret crush on Raul, never mind that he's married."

Anna opened her mouth to comment, but I beat

her to it. "And then the four of you ran into Benjamin?"

Carl nodded. "Why, yes. Exactly." He seemed impressed I'd put two and two together. It wasn't so much that, as simply trying not to spend all day in Cabin and Hearth without ever getting back to the matter at hand. "The four of us were milling about, Lucy constantly stubbing her toe on something or other and making noises, when I saw Benjamin and Petra talking to Owen and Silas. They were doing a better job than my group at being quiet, but from the expression on their faces, it looked like they were having a heated conversation."

I thought maybe I'd heard wrong. "You saw Silas with them?"

He nodded again.

"And you didn't see Myrtle with Silas?" The last time Katie and I had seen Silas, he'd been with Myrtle, and Benjamin was nowhere to be found.

Carl seemed to consider, his eyes narrowing. "No, I don't think so."

So Benjamin wasn't Myrtle's alibi, like Katie had expected, nor was Silas like I'd figured. Granted, if I was remembering all twelve of Myrtle's disciples, that left only Alice, Pete, Paulie, and Henry unaccounted for. And Henry ended up dead. So either

Pete, Paulie, or Alice had a chance to get Henry alone, or it was Myrtle. "How long was it before you heard Alice scream?"

Carl shrugged. "I'm not sure. Maybe five minutes, maybe ten or more. My group didn't join theirs. In fact, Roxanne and I ended up splitting from Raul and Lucy. We kept going farther back into the forest. Roxanne was convinced she saw the owl hopping from tree to tree, so I followed along. It turned out to be another mountain jay. How in the world a woman so good at bird trivia could mistake a jay for an owl, I'll never know."

Five to ten minutes, or more.... Anything could happen in that time. The people Carl's story truly cleared were Roxanne and himself.

Anna smacked Carl's arm again. "Well, that doesn't help at all. What a waste of time that story was!"

Carl gaped at her. "Well, I didn't say I solved the murder. I said I didn't see Benjamin with Myrtle."

"In that amount of time, Benjamin easily could have teamed up with Myrtle. What good did telling us all of that do?" Anna sounded thoroughly disgusted.

He pointed at me. "She asked."

Another thought hit me. "Wait a minute, Carl. You said that Lucy and Raul were together."

Carl glanced at Anna's hand before nodding.

"Well, like before, anything could've happened in the time you and Roxanne split up with them, but when Leo, Katie, and I heard the scream, I'm fairly certain we were the first ones on the scene. And Lucy and Alice were the only ones who were there." I thought back, trying to recreate the image. Maybe that wasn't true. Maybe Raul had been there as well, off in the shadows, out of sight.

Carl rolled his eyes. "As much as I can't stand Alice, the woman is no murderer. Obviously I don't have proof of that, but she just isn't."

That was similar to how I felt about Myrtle. "Why can't you stand Alice?"

"I *earned* my badges. Every single one." Carl tapped his chest as if he was wearing his vest in counting the badges. "I practice my birdcalls religiously."

"I can attest to that." Anna grimaced. "Twenty minutes a day." She smacked the glass countertop. "Twenty. Minutes. A day. Twenty! Of the most horrid squeaking and squawking noises you've ever heard, outside of Myrtle herself, that is."

Percival snorted. "You got that right. That

woman can squawk with the best of them. Maybe that's how she killed Henry."

"You don't like her because she got on to you for chasing that bird with a broom." Gary shook his finger at Percival as he would a naughty child. "Just because the two of you don't see eye to eye doesn't mean she's a murderer."

I tried to rein it in before I lost complete control once more. "What do you mean, Carl? How does Alice get her badges?"

"She cheats!" True indignation crossed his features. "The woman never travels. Ever. So how did she get a recording of the kakapo screeching? The bird is in New Zealand."

"Maybe she went to the zoo, or got it off YouTube." Gary sounded like he was trying to be helpful.

Carl apparently felt otherwise, judging from his stern expression. "That would still be cheating, though, wouldn't it? A badge for capturing bird sounds is only valid if caught in the wild. Nothing in captivity, and you have to capture it yourself. Same is true for the badge for having the most photos." He shook his head.

Gary tried again. "Well, I know Alice has a son

who's going to school to be a sound designer for movies. Maybe he makes them for her."

"That is still cheating!" This time, he smacked the counter, only to receive a second smack from Anna.

"You're going to break the glass." She smacked him a third time.

"So Henry's accusations of people cheating were true." Maybe whoever killed him didn't do so because he accused them of poaching, but simply was one of the other cheaters. It seemed a rather drastic reason for murder, but for people willing to pay ten thousand a year to be in a club, maybe not....

"Henry accused everyone of everything." Carl scoffed. "He even accused me of cheating on my sounds, saying that I had a recording in my pocket and was opening my mouth while I hit Play. Horrible man. But when you accuse everyone of everything, you're bound to land on the truth every once in a while."

Yes, I'd heard that logic about Henry before as well. But still... some of Carl's words replayed in my mind. "Wait a minute. Did you say Alice got a badge for having the sound of a kakapo?"

"Yes, I did. But she's gotten badges for sounds of

lots of birds. But that one was the most infuriating, since that's Myrtle's favorite bird."

I gaped at him. "The kakapo is Myrtle's favorite bird?"

"Oh, yes." Carl was all seriousness. "She loves all birds, but none of them as much as a kakapo. Which, I can't blame her. They are rather fascinating creatures. But if you're going to cheat, it's a little gross to go that extra mile toward brown-nosing the teacher, basically."

"Hold on." Percival reached out and grabbed Carl's arm. "Are you telling me Myrtle Bantam's favorite bird is called a kakapo. As in caca and poo. Her favorite bird is named after two types of poop?" He threw back his head and nearly peed himself laughing.

At that point, I knew I'd completely and utterly lost any chance of getting more actual information from any of them.

NINE

I checked my cell as Watson and I stepped back out onto Elkhorn Avenue. No text. Either Katie was still talking to Myrtle, or she truly had been sucked down the Google hole of random kakapo trivia. I glanced toward Myrtle's store at the other end of the street. I was tempted to go there. If Katie was already talking to her, then the ice would be broken. If nothing else, maybe I could get her to accidentally let slip what happened after she and Silas had left us that night. Although with my luck, I'd say something to irritate Myrtle and damage any relationship Katie was managing to build.

No, I needed to trust that Katie knew what she was doing.

The thought of Katie made me realize that the two owners of the Cozy Corgi bookshop and bakery had abandoned their store to someone who'd worked there for less than a day.

I glanced at Watson. "Sammy is pretty much a creepy clone of Katie, which means she can handle just about anything. We're good, right? It's not like anybody was buying books anyway."

Watson flicked an ear in my direction.

"Exactly. She's got it all under control. We'll drop by Myrtle's and see... no. No, we won't." I motioned toward the other end of the street. "We'll go to Alice's candle store, see if we can get her to talk about cheating. Though how I'm going to do that, I have no idea." With the sun sinking lower, the January afternoon was getting cooler, and I adjusted my mustard-hued scarf a little closer. "Okay, decision made, let's go."

Watson followed and let out a little bark as we neared the end of the block.

I turned back to him and found Watson staring at the door to Black Bear Roaster. Despite devouring his dog treat from Anna, Watson was doubtlessly picturing the countless too-dry scones we'd purchased there before Katie had opened the bakery. "Oh no, we're not going in there. I'm sure Carla is furious at whatever business Katie's taking away.

Besides, you don't need another parched scone, do you?"

He whimpered.

We had a staring contest for a minute. I lost, as always. I wasn't sure why I bothered. Admitting defeat, I shielded my eyes with my hands, and pressed against the window, trying to see if Carla was behind the counter. She wasn't. Feeling better, I started to pull away, and then noticed someone waving. Carla, holding a baby, sat at the table by the window, less than a few inches away from where I'd smashed myself against the glass. I jerked back, then offered the most awkward wave in the history of waving.

I glared at Watson. "This is your fault. You and your love of bone-dry baked goods. It's not like I can walk away now."

For his part, Watson gave a little hop as I reached for the front door, but looked thwarted when I paused by the first table to the right. "Carla. It's so nice to see you." Suddenly I remembered the baby in her arms. "Oh, you had your baby." I leaned closer. He wasn't the cutest of babies, but newborns rarely were. "He's adorable!"

"This is Shayla, and she's a girl." Carla simultaneously shifted baby Shayla in her arms, exposing her ever-growing belly, and motioned to the woman I'd not even noticed sitting across from her. "She's Tiffany's little girl, and I still have one more month until I'm due."

"Oh!" I attempted a smile toward Tiffany. "Well, Shayla is absolute... perfection." I cleared my throat. "I don't want to take up your time. I'm sure you're busy. We just came in for a coffee and a scone."

Carla's eyebrows shot so far up they were hidden behind her blonde bangs. "Really? Can't you get that at your store? Are you already tired of Katie's inferior baking?"

At any other time, I would've defended Katie with every ounce of fire my long auburn hair bestowed upon me, but I'd already stuck my foot in my mouth too many times in the matter of ten seconds. "Nope. Just had a craving for chai, and Watson loves your scones."

Figuring out that heaven was near as I said his name, Watson gave another little hop.

At that point, I was certain Carla would never be able to find her eyebrows again. "Your *dog* loves my scones?"

Synapses stopped firing as I tried to figure out if it was better to make a purchase or throw myself out the front door. "Watson has a very discerning palate."

And with that, I turned and led Watson to the counter, instantly knowing that I'd chosen the wrong option. Even so, I ordered a dirty chai and a blueberry scone.

I could feel Carla's eyes drilling into my back. Perhaps it didn't take the kid two hours to make the chai, but it sure felt like it. Maybe it wasn't too late to run out the front door.

As I waited, a conversation wafted through the buzzing in my brain. "I'm telling you, there's nothing to worry about. They don't have anything on Myrtle."

At Myrtle's name, I turned around, and apparently not only had I lost the art of having an intelligent conversation with someone without accidentally being insulting, but I'd also forgotten how to not be obvious.

"You gotta quit calling me. She's going to be—" The man was sitting at a nearby table, and his words fell away as our eyes met.

It took me a second to put a name with his face. And when I did, I gave a little wave. "Hi, Owen." Well, look at that. It appeared I'd outdone myself on the world's most awkward wave. I was on a roll.

His expression brightened instantly, and he didn't lower the phone as he spoke. "Fred Page. Imagine running into you here." He glanced at Watson, but didn't offer comment. "Awful business the other night. But I heard you found a pretty little pin to turn in to the police." Though his lips formed what I thought was meant to be a smile, I felt a chill.

"You know, I heard that rumor, in fact—"

The barista cut me off, thankfully. "Large dirty chai and blueberry scone for Fred, on the counter."

I glanced back at the voice, and, for some stupid reason, gave a third wave to the teenage barista. "Thank you!" I'd never meant those words more. I gave a brave attempt at a smile to Owen, without meeting his eyes. "Well, that's me. Watson and I should be off. Nice running into you." I whirled, and practically dragged Watson across the floor as I scooped up the chai and the scone and booked it out the door. I didn't stop until we were two stores down.

Watson let out a huff, clearly affronted.

"Don't give me that attitude. You're the reason I went in there, remember? That was all your fault. All of it. Granted you didn't lift up both my feet and shove them in my mouth and down my throat, but still." I let out a sigh. "Seriously, what was that? Sometimes I wonder if Barry is secretly my real father." I shuddered at that thought and started to hand the scone to Watson, then remembered he'd just had a large all-natural dog treat. I'd given up on the diet I'd placed him on the month before. He'd lasted a whole ten minutes on it anyway. Even so, I broke the scone in half and handed a portion to him. I took a bite of the other, discovered the scone was still as dry as the Sahara, and despite my hatred of wasting food, tossed it in a nearby trash can.

I stood there, stunned, sipping my chai, hoping the caffeine would take effect and reset my brain. Someone was worried about Myrtle, and apparently was repeatedly calling Owen about it. Maybe it hadn't been simply one person responsible for killing Henry. Maybe it had been three. And maybe I was completely wrong about my gut feeling about Myrtle.

Watson finished devouring his scone, and looked at my empty hand, clearly expecting the other half.

Before I could remind him that I would be a horrible corgi mama if I allowed him to overdose on sugar, Owen stepped out of the coffee shop and, miracle of miracles, walked in the other direction without even looking our way.

Even so, I wasn't going to press my nonexistent luck, and I hurried toward Alice's candle shop, though I wasn't sure there was any point after over-hearing that conversation. At least Watson and I were off the streets and out of Owen's possible view.

There was a chime as we entered Mountain Scents.

Alice, and an older Asian woman, both looked my way from the counter, straightened, and offered smiles that clearly stated I'd interrupted their conver-sation. When Alice spoke, her tone was entirely too cheerful. "Fred! And Watson! Petra and I haven't seen you since the hike the other night. I'm still shaken up about it."

For some reason, I hadn't recognized Petra as one of the members of the Feathered Friends Brigade. She nodded and found her voice. "Yes, we were talking about how awful it was. Poor Henry."

Though I didn't have a specific reason why, my gut told me they were lying. Although, maybe I was thrown off from my interaction with Owen and prone to suspect everyone at this point. "Yes, it was quite shocking." I took a sip of my chai, trying to figure out what to say, and then gave the cup a dirty look.

Alice laughed, this time the sound seeming authentic. "It's all the candles." She waved her hand in a circular motion in the air, encompassing the hundreds upon hundreds of candles in the store. "All the smells at once change the taste of nearly everything. I don't notice it anymore, but when I first opened, I thought it was the best diet plan I'd ever had."

Thank goodness Katie had wanted to open a bakery in the top floor of the Cozy Corgi, and not a candle shop. "That's kinda fascinating. I'll try not to take too much of your time so my chai doesn't get cold before I can drink it without it tasting like lavender." For some reason I thought that would be a joke, but it fell flat.

"You should try owning an ice cream parlor. I gave up on diets thirty years ago." If Petra was attempting humor, it felt as flat as mine had.

The three of us stared at each other awkwardly, and I could feel Watson's judgment. And I had to admit, by that point, it was well deserved.

"Did you come in for a candle?" Though she smiled, Alice seemed as ready to get the show on the road as I was.

This had been a mistake. At least so soon after my interaction with Carla and Owen. I needed time to process through things. And to remove my foot from my mouth, where it seemed stubbornly affixed. I decided to be honest. I wasn't capable of pulling off anything else convincingly at this point. "No, I actually came by to talk about the other night. I was wondering what you ladies noticed in the forest." I shrugged at Petra. "Well, I didn't know you were here, but that was the luck of the draw. Two birds with one stone, I suppose."

Both of their eyes widened again, and it took me a heartbeat to realize that I'd received confirmation that my foot was indeed still in my mouth. One does not reference killing birds with stones to ornithological-obsessed people. Especially when one of their own had been murdered.

"Sorry. You know what I mean." That was doubtful. At this point even I didn't know what I meant anymore.

"Aren't the police investigating Henry's death? I did hear that you found one of Myrtle's pins at the scene, but aren't they taking it from there?" From Alice's tone, I was certain there was going to be a call to the police as soon as I walked out the door.

I attempted to skate around that question. "It's just that... Katie is thinking about joining." Turned out I was wrong. The truth wasn't going to cut it. And even as I continued, I knew the lie would fall flat, as everything else had. I should dial Branson and hand them the phone to get it over with already. "I know that Katie is an adult and able to make her own decisions, but for some reason, I feel protective. And I don't know if joining a club where someone was murdered, most likely by someone in that club, since we were the only ones up there, is the best idea. So... I thought I'd ask you, as two other women, how safe you feel."

They stared at me.

"Well, you know, with all the talk of poaching and everything. I don't want Katie to get mixed up in something." I should've followed Alice and Petra's lead and kept my mouth shut. "If there is a poacher turned murderer in the group, I don't think it's a good idea for her to join."

"Poacher?" Petra flinched, her gaze darkening. "You know, maybe it's bad to speak ill of the dead, but you shouldn't give a word Henry said a bit of credence." For a second it looked like she was about to launch into a sermon, then she sniffed and gave an apologetic glance toward Alice. "You know, I've been gone from the ice cream parlor too long as it is." She hurried past Watson and me with another glare and out the door.

I'd not meant to hit a nerve, or even to imply anything, but it seemed as far as Petra was concerned, I'd done both. And it felt like it was more than me sticking my foot in my mouth. I focused on Alice, hoping I'd not already managed to shut her down. "Sorry, I know I interrupted yours and Petra's conversation. I can come back later if you'd like."

Alice hesitated, and when she spoke, her words were slow and deliberate. "Fred, you are always welcome in my store. But I'm not sure what you're looking for here. I sell candles, that's it. In my spare time, I enjoy bird-watching and gathering with like-minded people. I don't have any clues to give you."

"No, I told you, I'm here because...." I let the words fade away. It was pointless. And even though I knew anything else I could possibly say would also be pointless, this was clearly the one chance I would have. Once I walked out the door, I was certain she really would call the police, and probably never speak to me again. So, once more, I tried for the truth. I reminded myself that I was Percival's niece, so I opted for the blunt truth.

"Honestly, Alice, you're right. I am here because of Henry's murder. Henry, as Petra demonstrated, made a lot of enemies. Constantly accusing other members of the group of cheating or poaching, and who knows what else." As I spoke the truth, some of my confidence came back. "In talking to other people who are in the club, your name came up as someone

Henry was right about." I nearly stopped there but decided to push a little further, milk the chance for everything it had since it would be my last. "It seems his accusations about you cheating to earn your badges were true." Though the next part was speculation, I decided to take the risk. "Some are saying that you've gotten your son involved in your cheating. That he's provided you fake recordings from the school in Denver where he is studying to work on sound in movies."

"It's bad enough you imply Petra might have something to do with Henry's death." All timidness fell away, as did any hint of friendliness in her tone. "But don't you dare bring my son into this. He was not in those woods that night."

I flinched, completely thrown off. "I wasn't saying he was, Alice. Simply that he's helping you cheat to earn your badges."

"So what?" She sneered, her lips curling over her teeth, reminding me of what people said about mother bears. I'd not meant to threaten her son, but it seemed she was taking it that way. "They're a few badges. Pieces of embroidered fabric. Nothing to kill someone over. If you want to go around accusing other people, then I suggest you talk to Benjamin, ask him how he helped Silas get all his." She began to walk around the counter, and despite being several inches taller than her, I backed up in the face of her fury. "How dare you think that my son or I would murder someone for a bunch of stupid badges." She thrust out both her hands at me. "Get out of here. You and your dirty little dog. Get out of my store."

She didn't have to tell me twice.

TEN

The shelter of the Cozy Corgi was in sight when I noticed Katie hurrying down the sidewalk from the other direction, her eyes bright with excitement. I bypassed the entrance to the bookshop to meet her, having to pause a moment to pull Watson away from the front door. He was either ready to get in from the cold or simply tired of seeing his mama make a fool of herself.

Katie grasped my hand as we met, and her voice was breathless. "How did things go for you? Any luck?"

I winced. "Judging from your expression, I'm guessing you had a better go of it than me. Why don't you start? You were with Myrtle for quite a while."

"Well, I probably spent longer researching that kakapo bird than I truly needed to, but I'm glad I did. Mentioning it to her was like opening Pandora's box." Though still excited, her giddy smile softened slightly. "You know, I genuinely like her. Granted, she's a little obsessive and strange, but so am I. Personally, I think both of those are redeeming qualities."

I rather thought so myself. And despite Myrtle's and my tense relationship, the more time I spent with her, the more I liked her as well. Although after hearing Owen's phone call, I wasn't sure I could trust my gut. "I hope you're right. But what did she say about Benjamin?"

"Well...." Katie hesitated for a second. "She was careful about what she said regarding Benjamin, honestly. I couldn't get a good read on why. She wouldn't say that she wasn't with Benjamin when Henry was killed, but she didn't say that she was either."

"What does that mean?" A large man bumped into my shoulder without apology as he tried to step around Katie, Watson, and me. I motioned toward the wooden bench affixed in the sidewalk close to the street. "Actually, why don't we sit? I know there's not too many tourists wandering around downtown, but we're still kinda in the way."

Katie followed me to the bench. After glaring for a few seconds, Watson curled up underneath, between our feet. "I think it means she wasn't with him. But she's not exactly going to tell me that, is she? Not if Benjamin is her alibi. And not if she feels protective of him."

"So, between what you felt when you spoke to Benjamin and now with Myrtle, and combine that with what Carl told me, I think we can safely assume Benjamin is indeed lying to cover for Myrtle." At Katie's confused expression, I remembered I hadn't filled her in yet. "Oh, sorry. Carl suggested that he saw Benjamin with other people in the woods. Although, there was a gap in time that doesn't make what he saw very helpful. But combined with what you're feeling, I'd say it's accurate."

"But I still don't think Myrtle killed Henry. Maybe Benjamin is just trying to protect her or her reputation, not helping her get away with murder."

I filled her in on what I'd overheard from Owen's phone call.

Katie looked less certain. "Whoever he was talking to is worried about the police having enough evidence to pin on Myrtle?"

"It seems that way, if I understood what he was saying. Granted, it was one side of the conversation, but it seemed pretty clear." We had to be missing something important, although the simplest answer was that Myrtle was the one who killed Henry. Even if I didn't understand why. "I think I've been assuming that the reason Henry got killed was somehow connected to the poaching. It doesn't make sense for someone to kill Henry over his accusations about cheating over badges, even if he was obnoxious and abrasive." I relayed the interactions I'd had with Alice and Petra. "Whatever's going on, I think there's a lot more to the Feathered Friends Brigade than weekly meetings and badges. Though I can't tell if it's one big thing that everyone's in on, or whether several different secrets jumbled together ended up getting Henry killed."

Katie's expression darkened as I told her about what Alice said regarding Benjamin and Silas. "It sounds like we can definitely assume there's a lot of cheating happening, if nothing else. Not to mention that Henry wasn't half as crazy as he seemed. And if Benjamin is willing to lie to the police to cover for Myrtle, I'd say Alice's accusation is not too far a stretch."

"I agree."

"Oh, I forgot." Katie smacked her thigh. "It was the very first thing Myrtle said to me, but I was more taken aback by how she responded about Benjamin. She says the kakapo pin wasn't hers. She had never seen it until the police showed it to her during questioning."

That made absolutely no sense. "Really? I'd swear it's the exact same style as the one she gave you."

Katie nodded. "It is. She said that it was done by the same artist who creates her pins. A Native American artist in Santa Fe."

"She honestly expects people to believe she collects those pins yet doesn't have one of her favorite bird?" Maybe I was reading Myrtle wrong.

"According to Myrtle, she hasn't earned it yet."

"She hasn't *earned* it?"

"No." Katie shook her head, and her tone softened. "It's kinda sweet. Or something. Myrtle only allows herself to get pins of birds she's interacted with. She's never seen a kakapo in real life. She's saving up for a trip to New Zealand to visit a sanctuary for them. She was going to get the pin after that, sort of like a reward, I guess, or memento."

It was plausible, I supposed, but still.... "A woman who charges ten grand a year to be part of a bird club doesn't have enough money to take a trip to New Zealand?"

Katie shrugged. "I think that simply proves she's not mismanaging the money. She's dogmatic about raising funds to save birds, Fred. I don't think one penny goes to anything else. Even the check she used when she paid for me catering the other night was from her personal account. Not the bird club or her shop."

Though it was hard to believe, if the pin truly didn't belong to Myrtle, that did change things. It seemed too much of a coincidence for someone else to simply be wearing one of Myrtle's style of pins, losing it, right by the scene of Henry's murder. Although, if they were attempting to frame her, why didn't they put it closer to the body?

"Hey! There you two are!"

Katie and I both looked toward the voice, and saw Sammy leaning out the front door of the Cozy Corgi.

"What in the world are you two doing? I'm dying in here. I'm having people bring books up that they want to buy to the bakery, but I have no idea what I'm doing."

Katie sprang up. "I'm so sorry! I'll be right there."

Sammy slammed the door without any further response.

Katie grinned at me. "Did you hear that? People are buying books."

"Apparently, all it takes is for me to not be there."

I stood, and we took a few paces toward the shop, when I paused. "You know, if you don't mind handling things for a little bit longer, I think I should go talk to Benjamin right now. If my instincts are right, Alice has already called the police, telling them I'm harassing her or something. And it's only a matter of time before Branson shows up. I don't want to miss my chance." I held out Watson's leash. "Would you take him with you? I'm pretty sure if we go anywhere else, he'll murder me in my sleep tonight."

"Of course. Good idea." I could tell from her expression that Katie was disappointed she wasn't getting to go to Benjamin as well, but she took Watson's leash. "Come on, buddy. I've got a dog bone with your name all over it."

I started to object as they walked away; he'd already had two sizable treats in the past hour. But he'd probably earned it. And I could give him the equivalent of a doggy salad that evening to compensate.

Yeah, right. Only if I truly did want to get murdered in my sleep.

I started to check my phone, figuring I'd already missed a call from Branson, then decided to leave well enough alone. That way I could claim genuine ignorance if it all blew up in my face. As if feeling him hot on my trail, I glanced around. The coast was clear, so I hurried down the sidewalk toward the camera shop.

As I entered Shutterbug, Benjamin noticed me instantly. He was demonstrating a camera that looked about a foot long, to a couple of customers, and his spiel faltered. He swallowed and then forced a smile and continued showing the couple the features of the camera.

My heart sank a bit. This wasn't going to go well. I hadn't even had a chance to put my foot in my mouth, and he already looked one step away from kicking me out.

I considered leaving. Why waste more time, or possibly have one more person making complaints about me to the police? But it felt like my only chance to talk to him.

His gaze flitted my way as he closed the sale and began to ring up the customers. Benjamin looked on the verge of bolting.

For him to be having such a strong reaction, someone must have alerted him that I might show up. Maybe Alice had called him the minute I left. However, I doubted it. The way she'd told me about him helping Silas cheat hadn't felt like she cared enough to warn him. If it got any attention off her and her son, she might happily throw Benjamin under the bus to do it. Maybe Owen had called.

I worked my way closer as they finished up the transaction, hoping it would make it less likely Benjamin would turn and hightail it out of the store. I nearly choked when I heard the final price of the camera equipment they bought. It suddenly made a lot more sense why he might pay ten thousand a year if he had a steady stream of camera sales from the bird club. Although it seemed to me once a person bought a camera, they were probably done for several years, if not forever. But maybe they were now like cell phones, with constant updates and endless demands to have the newest and best in technology.

As soon as the customers were gone, Benjamin turned to me. Though younger, there was something about Benjamin that reminded me of Branson. Nearly as handsome, and I got the feeling, typically as charming. Though it seemed he hadn't quite mastered that aspect yet, at least when nervous.

Maybe give him a few years. "I heard you were making the rounds."

That was all the confirmation I needed. "I'm simply trying to figure out what happened." This time I opted for a combination of truth and fiction. Or at least an exaggerated version of the truth. "I'm the one who found Myrtle's pin, and I feel responsible. I don't think she's a killer, and I'd hate for something I did to implicate her if she's innocent."

His shoulders sagged in relief. "It won't. She was with me. Haven't you heard? I talked to the police this morning. Myrtle's probably at her store right now."

I leveled a gaze on him that I'd used during my years of being a professor when I was certain a student was lying about why they couldn't complete a project or had been caught cheating. "Benjamin, everyone knows that's not true. Well, not the police, *yet*; give them time. But like you said, I've been making my rounds. Your name has come up more than once." I moved a little closer, drawing up to my full height, not necessarily to look threatening, just authoritarian. "About several things."

Like it had with my students, the move worked. "Several things?" His voice squeaked.

"Yes. One of which is that you were seen with

other people at the time of the murder. With Petra, I believe. Not Myrtle."

He licked his lips but didn't speak. The wheels in his brain were turning so quickly I could nearly see them behind his eyes. In that moment, Benjamin seemed even younger than I'd thought, and I decided to use a touch of intimidation. "I don't know how much you know about me, but I'm fairly close to Sergeant Wexler, and my father was a detective. I've seen how this plays out many times throughout my life, Benjamin. It never ends well when you're lying to the police."

"What happens?" His eyes got so wide, I almost felt guilty. Benjamin shook his head, as if realizing what he'd said. "Not that I was lying."

"The thing is"—I leaned against the counter, this time trying to take on a motherly tone—"it's kind of like with your parents when you're a kid. When you're caught, things go easier for you if you're honest about it as opposed to continuing the lie. That only makes things bigger and bigger."

"But this wasn't a bad lie. Myrtle wouldn't kill anybody. She didn't."

His admission was so sudden that it nearly threw me off, and it didn't even seem he'd realized what he'd implied. "Then who did, Benjamin? If you know Myrtle didn't commit murder, who did?"

"I don't know!" He threw up his hands. "I really don't. But Myrtle wouldn't do that. Maybe I wasn't with her, but she wouldn't kill anyone."

"So you were simply trying to protect Myrtle?"

He swallowed. "Yeah."

His hesitation was long enough to let me know he was lying, again. "Tell me the truth, Benjamin. Who told you to be Myrtle's alibi?"

"He did it because he loves her. He couldn't handle seeing her taken into custody." Benjamin's words were nearly slurred in his panic. "And it's not a crime, at least not a bad one. He and I are both certain that Myrtle wouldn't kill anyone."

"Who, Benjamin? Who's in love with Myrtle?"

"Silas." He looked at me as if the answer was obvious, and then his eyes widened once more, finally realizing how much he'd shared. "I swear, Fred. It really is okay. Silas loves her. He was trying to protect her, and you said yourself, you know Myrtle would never do anything like that. I'm not lying to cover up a murder. Just to... protect the innocent."

I was so thrown off at the revelation that Silas was having a relationship with Myrtle that I nearly lost my train of thought. I wasn't even sure why the couple seemed like such an odd pairing to me, but they did. For whatever reason, I couldn't picture Myrtle in a relationship with anyone. But I could think on that later. I'd cracked Benjamin. I needed to keep pounding, as uncomfortable as it was, to see what else I could get. "Speaking of Silas, I also heard that you assist him, and maybe even some other members when they require certain photo work done to help them earn badges."

At that, he relaxed, and waved me off. "That's not a big deal either. Silas really has seen all those birds. I simply doctor the photos a little bit. That's not cheating."

"Doctor them? If Silas has seen the birds, why doctor the photos?"

For whatever reason, that question changed everything. Benjamin straightened, and his eyes grew cold. "I think I've said too much to you the way it is. This isn't your business. And no harm has been done. Myrtle wouldn't do that. If I thought she could kill someone, it wouldn't matter what Silas offered. I would never cover for a murderer. Ever."

Whether he was right about Myrtle or not, I heard the truth in his words, but I caught something else as well. "Why? What did Silas offer you to cover for Myrtle?"

He flinched, and I thought he was about to crack again, but he didn't. "Nothing. I didn't say he did. I was... saying that it wouldn't matter what he *might* offer. I wouldn't cover for a murderer."

"Benjamin, I think it's in your best interest if you're completely honest right now. What did—"

"No." Benjamin shook his head. "I think you need to leave. And if you believe that Myrtle is innocent like I do, like you said you did, you'll leave it alone." The way his voice quavered at the end led me to believe he was more worried about the police showing up to talk to him about his lying than he was about Myrtle.

For the second time in less than an hour, I walked back out into the January afternoon after being kicked out of another store. The shadows were growing long, and the charming little downtown suddenly felt ominous.

It was too much at once. The phone call I'd overheard from Owen, the revelation that Silas and Myrtle were in a relationship, Petra and Alice's reactions, and the constant confirmation that most of Henry's claims were true after all.

My cell vibrated in my pocket, and I pulled

it out.

A glance at the screen revealed the call I'd expected. Just a little later than I would've anticipated.

I hesitated with my thumb hovering over Branson's name, then hit Decline and put the phone back in my pocket. I had to figure things out before I spoke to him. All I needed now was him lecturing or threatening, and not only would I lose my temper, but I might miss my chance to try to arrange the puzzle pieces in a way that made sense while the information was clear.

As my phone began to buzz again, I knew what Branson's next step would be. Ignoring the cell entirely, I hurried back toward the Cozy Corgi. I should pick up Watson before Branson showed up at the bookshop. I probably wouldn't go home either, as he'd likely show up there as well. Whatever. I'd figure that out later. Right now I'd grab my corgi, hop in my car, and avoid the police.

ELEVEN

Branson called and texted nearly ten times in the next half hour. I started by driving randomly around Estes Park, then realized I had a high chance of accidentally running into him as he drove to the Cozy Corgi or to my house. So Watson and I made our way into the national park. It was a stunning night for a drive to clear my head, and I highly doubted he would look for me there.

Though I still couldn't picture Myrtle as a murderer, she truly seemed the most likely of suspects. She was the founder of the club, a group with a limitless supply of secrets and cheating. Her story about the pins to Katie was rather sweet and something I could see someone with Myrtle's disposition doing, but all fingers pointed to her. The solitary reason to believe otherwise was my gut instinct. And as much as I'd learned to trust my gut recently, I didn't believe it was infallible.

If it had been Myrtle, I highly doubted she'd acted alone. There were too many secrets in the club for it to come down to one person. But then again, that was another gut feeling without much basis in anything substantial, besides endless rumors and gossip and accusations. Which in the Feathered Friends Brigade, seemed like it led to getting killed if you talked about them too much.

If nothing else, it seemed Owen had a reason to cover for Myrtle. And Silas as well. I wasn't sure what deal Silas had struck with Benjamin, but I was certain the kid hadn't done it out of his own pure heart. Though I did believe he wouldn't cover for Myrtle if he truly thought she'd killed Henry. But there I went again, nothing but gut instinct to back that up, and I'd had even less interaction with Benjamin than with Myrtle.

Then there was Alice and Petra. Surely Alice wouldn't kill someone because they knew her son was helping her cheat to get badges. And I couldn't imagine what secrets Petra might be keeping, but she'd been so clearly uncomfortable in my presence. They both had. Although, maybe that was more about me than about either of them.

Atypically, Watson wasn't curled up napping in the front seat, but sat up tall, which put his gaze right at the edge of the passenger-side window, allowing him to see the dark silhouettes of the snowy trees as we passed. Maybe he'd enjoyed the snowy moonlight hike the night before and hoped we were going to do it again.

The night before... had it only been twenty-four hours ago? It felt like days. I'd talked to so many people and been kicked out of so many stores. I chuckled at the thought, causing Watson to glance over with a look that asked, "Why is my mother such a nut ball?" before turning back to stare out the window.

And in those twenty-four hours, and the whirlwind of questions to everyone, all I had to show for my effort was alienating myself further from Branson, and Susan, for that matter, not that it took much. That, and a whole bunch of loose ends that didn't seem to lead anywhere.

When my phone rang again, this time from an unknown number, I'd had enough. Keeping my eyes on the road, I hit Accept and lifted the phone to my ear. "Seriously? It's not enough to harass me from your own number, now you're trying to trick me?" Even as I said the words, I heard the ridiculousness of them. The trick had worked. Though maybe not so much a trick as him simply knowing at some point my temper would take over.

"Winifred Page?" The voice was not Branson Wexler.

"Oh... sorry." I couldn't believe I could still speak after shoving my foot in my mouth on so many occasions in one day. Surely this had to be a record. "This is Winifred. I thought you were someone else. Sorry about that." Then I realized it might not be Branson, but I had no idea who I was talking to. "Speaking of, who is this?"

"Silas Belle." There was laughter in his tone. "Sounds like you're having a harassment issue. Might need to call the police about that."

I pulled the phone back and looked at the screen. That had been an odd thing to say, an oddly apt thing to say, letting me know that Silas knew exactly what he was talking about. I brought the phone back to my ear once more and focused on not letting the wary sensation I felt sound in my voice. "Not a bad idea. What can I help you with, Silas?"

"I hear you've been all over town today, asking a lot of questions about Myrtle and the club." Impressively he was able to say the line without losing an ounce of warmth.

If he could be blunt, so could I. It seemed pointless to deny anything. Doubtlessly, Benjamin had called him. Alice, I wasn't so sure of, but possibly. "That's true. I have."

"Anything you want to ask me, Fred?"

My heart began to pound, and for an insane moment, I glanced at the rearview, expecting to see headlights trailing me. I wasn't in a horror movie, however. And unless Silas had a ton of forethought, he hadn't put a tracker on my car or my phone. "Yes, actually." I swallowed, then barged ahead. "I don't know what you used for motivation, but I do know that you convinced Benjamin to be Myrtle's alibi."

There were several heartbeats of silence, and when Silas spoke again, some of the warmth had faded, but he didn't sound necessarily angry. "It seems money talks only so far to Benjamin. I probably shouldn't have put such a large task in the hands of a man so young and inexperienced." He chuckled. "No offense to your grilling tactics, I'm sure."

I wasn't certain if I should be worried that he'd admitted it so easily or if it implied Myrtle truly was innocent.

Silas didn't wait. "I don't know if this is a conversation that's best over the phone. How about we meet in person? We're neighbors, after all. Would you like to come to my house, or should I come to yours?"

I waited for the punch line. There didn't seem to be one coming. "Silas, you might be the nicest man in the world. I don't know. But I promise you I'm not such a fool that I would go to someone's house, in the dark, to talk about this."

"Bring someone. I promise you there's no malin-tent on my end." The warmth was back, and he almost sounded nonchalant. Which only proved he was very much in control. "Bring several someones if you want. My singular request is that they not be law enforcement. I don't have any intention of admitting to them that I encouraged Benjamin to fake his alibi for Myrtle. And I believe after you hear me out, you'll understand why."

"And why can't we do this on the phone?" As if answering my own question, I drove through a thick grove of trees and the line went static for several moments.

Once the connection cleared, Silas continued speaking in his calm voice. "Deception is easy over the phone, Fred. If I'm going to convince you to not tell the police about my arrangement with Benjamin, I need you to believe me. And if I truly meant you any harm, I wouldn't have admitted it over the phone. You could drive straight to the police right now and fill them in, which is your right. But I hope that you won't."

He had a point, although that point could easily be simply to make me more willing to fall into his trap. I debated mentally, and as if he could hear me thinking, Silas didn't speak, giving me time to process.

I didn't think I had a ton of weaknesses, not anymore. Sure, my temper got the best of me every so often, and I could get flustered at times. And having a bakery right above my head was proving to be as problematic as I thought it would be for my diet. But hands down, my biggest fault was one of my biggest strengths. And even if I knew the saying *curiosity killed the cat*, I needed to have my fix. That curiosity craved to be satiated. "Fine."

As expected, Watson went positively wild when we pulled up to Leo's apartment. Leo was waiting in the parking lot. During my brief phone call with him, I requested for us to use his Jeep, less chance of accidentally running into Branson or Susan if they were scouring the area for me. Which, judging from the calls I was still getting from Branson, I imagined they were.

Leo held the door open for me as I scooped Watson into the Jeep, and then he hurried around to the driver's side and hopped in. In another second or so, we left the apartment complex and were heading toward my side of town.

"Gotta say, this is fun." Leo grinned his handsome smile at me as he looked away from the road for a second, childlike pleasure written across his features. "I feel like I'm in a Hardy Boys book."

I couldn't help but smile back, partly because I knew exactly the thrill shooting through him. "Actually, I think you're in a Nancy Drew book at the moment."

"Works for me." He tilted his head but didn't look back this time, keeping his gaze focused on the road. "Although, I'm pretty sure they did a few crossovers where the Hardy Boys teamed up with Nancy Drew. They were double digests, twice as long as the normal ones."

I gaped at him. "You read the Hardy Boys and Nancy Drew? You like mysteries?"

"Of course I did! And who doesn't like mysteries?"

And that answer was all the confirmation I

needed to know I'd made the right choice. Not that I'd questioned that choice to begin with. First and foremost, no matter how curious I was, I wasn't going to show up at Silas's house on my own. Nor was I going to call Branson. And not just because Silas had asked me not to. Leo had a relationship with Silas and all the members of the Feathered Friends Brigade. He would put Silas—hell, and me—at ease. And he'd also be better able to tell if Silas was being honest, since he had past experiences with him.

We weaved our way around the new developments of mini-mansions at the base of the mountain, nestled against the forest that held my cabin. The houses were beautiful and elaborate. And they felt completely out of place in Estes Park, like a portion of the rich suburbs had been plopped down among the pines.

We found the house number Silas had given me and Leo let out a whistle as we pulled into the driveway. "I knew the man had money, but he's got the biggest house on the block."

"You'd think with all that money, he could've afforded to build a custom cabin or something, as opposed to buying in Stepford."

"I knew I liked you." Leo flashed a smile but was smart enough to make it brief, then exited the Jeep.

I followed suit, grasping Watson's leash after I lowered him to the concrete.

Silas met us at the door before we even needed to ring the bell. "Well, well, my favorite ranger, Leo Lopez." He stuck out his hand, and the two men exchanged a handshake. He followed by giving me the same gesture. "Smart choice, Fred. Not alone, and someone that I know and trust. No wonder I've heard you're quite the detective."

My gut had been telling me lots of things the past several days, but it didn't help me out a lick with Silas's direct approach. I couldn't tell if he was letting me know he was aware of what I was doing to put me at ease or hint that he was several steps ahead.

The interior of Silas's house was as much of a mansion as the outside. He led us through a massive entrance with a sparkling chandelier hanging from a vaulted ceiling and past a formal dining room. Watson found some scent he loved on the floor in front of a closet door and required a tug on his leash to follow us. We continued into a kitchen-living room combo as big as my entire cabin. And like the housing development didn't fit the aesthetic of my little mountain town, neither did the interior of Silas's house. It reminded me of some of the home tours I'd taken in the Kansas City Plaza. Everything was black, cream, and tan, and decorated with glass and steel. Fine, I supposed. I'd been impressed during the home tour, at least. It all seemed luxurious and modern. But it felt wrong here, somehow. Like it expected the mountains to adjust to it instead of trying to blend in to the rugged wilderness mere feet away.

Leo grimaced or winced here and there, barely noticeable, but he was clearly having a similar response. That changed when we entered the large living room. He sucked in a quiet breath and walked over to a wall that could've been in a museum, filled with golden-framed canvases, each displaying a colorful bird. "These are spectacular. I feel like I'm stepping into a National Geographic." He let out a self-conscious laugh. "If the National Geographic was on Fifth Avenue."

"Thank you." Silas crossed the room and stood beside Leo, admiring the art as well. "It combines my two great loves, ornithology and photography." He cast a glance my way. "I've spent a small fortune on photography equipment. Benjamin is very accommodating." He chuckled. "More than a small fortune, I suppose."

I was surprised at the sudden mention of

Benjamin—it looked like we were starting. I'd wondered if Silas would be as direct in person as he had been over the phone. It seemed so. "Is that why Benjamin was willing to lie when you asked him to? Because you're such a great customer?"

Leo flashed me a wide-eyed look, clearly asking what I was thinking taking such a direct approach.

For Silas's part, he didn't even flinch. "No. Although, I'm sure that partly came into play for him. But, no. I paid Benjamin to say that he was with Myrtle. That time it had nothing to do with photography or cameras, or birds, for that matter." He left Leo's side, crossed the room once more, passed me, paused to pat Watson's head—who gave a half-hearted attempt at ducking away—and then pulled three wineglasses from a cupboard. "What can I get you? Are you two more red or white fans?"

He was so nonchalant that either he was crazy or truly had no worry that once we heard his story we'd believe him. Either way, it threw me off. And maybe that was the point.

"Thank you, Silas, but Fred and I aren't here for a drink." Leo moved from the wall of pictures and came to stand beside Watson and me.

"Well, let me know if you change your mind." Silas opened a bottle of red and poured himself a glass. He continued speaking as he got a small bowl and filled it with water and set it on the floor near Watson. "I'll be direct with you both. Like I told you on the phone, Fred, I can't stop you from going to the police and ruining Myrtle's alibi, but I hope that you will understand why I did what I did and respect my decision enough to let it stand. I don't know who killed Henry, but I have my suspicions. And even if those are wrong, I can guarantee you that Myrtle had absolutely nothing to do with it."

Two huge sofas made up most of the seating possibilities in the living room, one against the far wall and the other at an L-shape position, partially separating the living room from the kitchen space. Silas sat on the one next to the wall and gestured toward the other for Leo and me.

For a moment, he looked nervous for the first time. No... not nervous... I couldn't quite put my finger on it. Almost... in pain. His brown eyes met mine, then he glanced back and forth between the two of us, and finally settled on me. "I love Myrtle. I've been in love with her for years. She's the most amazing woman I've ever known. Her passion, dedication, and purity of heart and one-track mind. She is powerful and amazing. She would never harm another creature, even of the human variety." He swallowed, the pained look persisting. "That's why I paid Benjamin to be her alibi." He gestured around his house. "As you can see, I'm used to getting what I want. I've traveled the world several times over for my love of birds. I met Myrtle on a trip in Costa Rica on just such an expedition, and she blew me away. My life changed the day I met Myrtle Bantam. So you can't blame me if I'm willing to do whatever it takes to make sure she is safe, even if it means paying someone to lie for her. And you can understand why I might be a little bit worried that the story might crack somewhere and she'd get blamed again."

"You love her so much that you would cover for her even if she killed someone?"

Silas barely spared Leo a glance. "Don't be ridiculous. You know Myrtle; she didn't do this."

"I don't think she did it either, but sometimes people surprise us. And surely lying about it will only end up making her look guiltier." Leo's tender voice sounded like he was talking to a heartbroken teenager. It seemed he believed Silas's story of love. "Wouldn't it be better to simply let the police do their jobs?"

"It's a nice thought, but you don't really believe that, do you, Fred?" He looked to me though Leo had asked the question. "The whole town knows that you cleared your stepfather's name, and then your business partner." He cocked an eyebrow. "And here you are again. This time not even trying to clear someone you love. Simply not trusting the police to find the truth."

I couldn't think of anything to say but to agree. Before I needed to respond, Silas refocused on Leo.

"I only know Fred by reputation. But you I know, Leo. How have the police done with the bird club so far? Have they believed any of our theories about the poacher? Have they attempted to investigate? Have they even listened to you?"

Leo was struck as dumb as I was.

Silas looked back at me. "I admire you, Fred. You take matters into your own hands, and you protect the ones you love. I do that as well, though my manner in doing so is a little different. Maybe mine seems lazy to you, throwing money at things instead of investigating, but we each have our strengths. If anybody should understand what I'm doing, it's you."

I studied him, attempting to let my instincts and my brain work in tandem. I felt like they were. I believed him. Completely. From the look in his eyes and the sound of his voice, I had no doubt he loved Myrtle. And looking back, though I hadn't noticed it at the time and the actions weren't overt, the way he'd stood close to her, came to her defense. Always ready if she needed anything. As far as his way of going about it? I understood that too. Maybe it wasn't the way I would do it, but the result was the same. Though I would argue not as effective.

The bottom line was that my gut, as well as those of several people I trusted, told me Myrtle was innocent. And nearly every other person I'd spoken to dismissed the idea that Myrtle was capable of murder. The same had been true for Barry, and then again for Katie.

I was certain Myrtle wasn't going to break the pattern.

I couldn't blame Silas for what he was doing, even if I wished he'd chosen a different way. I nearly said as much, when another thought hit me. "If all that's true, Silas, I still don't understand why you would need to pay Benjamin to lie. Why not do it yourself? There'd have been no chance Benjamin would crack, like he did, and you could be her rock-solid alibi."

"I can't." Silas glanced away then, and a blush flared to his cheeks. When he finally looked back, though he couldn't meet my eyes as directly as before, I still believed him. "Myrtle doesn't know how I feel about her. And at this point, she can't know. It took months after I moved here for her to even speak to me. She thought I moved here for her, which I had, but it wasn't something she wanted. Myrtle doesn't want a relationship. Even her friendships are little more than an outreach for her passion of birds. It's an obsession. A lovely one, but an obsession nonetheless. One that leaves room for little else." He met my gaze again, holding it, and I could see the genuine desperation in his eyes. "She can't know. If she thought I had these sorts of feelings for her, she would cut me out. I don't think she'd let me be in the club anymore. If I was her alibi, she would ask why. I don't think I could do a good enough job of convincing her. But with Benjamin, she won't understand why, but she would never think of him loving her, not like she would if I'd proclaimed to be her alibi."

I glanced at Leo. And if I was reading his expression correctly, he believed Silas as well. Part of me wanted to ease Silas's worry, promise him I wouldn't tell Myrtle, but I wasn't going to jump quite that far. Still, I had every intention of keeping Silas's secret. I turned back to him, trying to keep my voice neutral. "You said you had some ideas of who might've killed Henry. What are they?"

Though I made no promises, I could see relief in Silas's eyes, and his shoulders relaxed. He sat back, sinking a little farther into the sofa. "They're nothing more than ideas. While I'm sure about Myrtle's innocence, I'm not sure about much else. It was Alice we heard scream. Seems like a good plan to me. Kill someone and be the first on the scene, screaming, crying, and shaken. Henry accused Alice of cheating, which I know she is, but still. He let it go for a few months, and then he returned, accusing her of cheating, then accusing her of being the poacher. My other thought was Paulie. I don't have that good of a reason to think it was him, other than he strikes me as a rather slimy little rat. And I know he'd been knocking on Henry's door—" He gave a sardonic chuckle. "—both literally and figuratively, trying to be his friend. The guy's like a little leech. Maybe Henry got tired of it, said something that hurt Paulie's feelings, and Paulie snapped." Silas shrugged. "They're speculation. In truth, while I was nervous to hear you were looking into things, I'm also glad of it, Fred. Whatever quality it is that helps a person figure out these kinds of things, I don't have it. You do, apparently. I can keep Myrtle out of jail with a fake alibi, but you can fully clear her name. Any resources you require, all you need to do is ask."

I thought I heard him wrong. "You want me to keep snooping?"

"Of course I do. Figure it out."

I hadn't expected that. I'd been saving the next question, planning to use it as my ace in the hole, to see if it would shake him at all. Now was the moment. "What about Myrtle's pin? I found it a few yards away from where Henry was killed."

Silas winced, the question clearly bothering him. "That wasn't Myrtle's pin. She only gets those when she's been with that bird species in the wild. Seeing the kakapo is her biggest dream. She'll get there one day, but she won't allow herself to have that pin until she does." He shrugged. "Again, I don't have an explanation, and for the life of me, I can't even come up with a plausible theory on that one. But I know it wasn't Myrtle's."

That fit perfectly with what Myrtle had told Katie, so either it was the truth or Silas and Myrtle were in it together. Though it felt like the truth.

I played my final card, which I'd been holding back, and motioned toward the wall of birds. "There're rumors that you cheat on your pictures."

He studied me again, then finally cast what I thought was an embarrassed look toward Leo. "I love Myrtle, and I'm as passionate about conservation as she is, but I'm not quite as strict as her thinking. Some of the birds I visited in other countries were in captivity. Not by poachers or anything like that—by people who had one of the native birds as their pets, or they were held in a local zoo. Benjamin adjusts those photos when that happens so they look like they're taken in the wild. That's all. Obviously I don't care about the stupid badges. But it gives me one more connection to Myrtle."

"Silas, just because someone lives in whatever area you're visiting, doesn't mean they have the bird legally and they're not poachers." Leo sounded somewhat aghast. "It would be no different than if we'd spotted a Mexican Spotted Owl the other night, captured it, and put it in a cage."

Silas shrugged at Leo. "Sorry. That's what I mean. I'm not quite as strict about these things as Myrtle. And I'd appreciate it if you keep that aspect of my story from her as well."

Leo looked like he was about to argue, but I had a feeling it was more about the birds and less about Myrtle. Which was fine, but he could do so on his own time.

"Silas, I'm not making any promises about what I will or won't say, both to Myrtle or the police. But I will consider what you said."

For a second, Silas seemed about to argue or push the point, but then he nodded. "Guess that's all I can expect." His eyes brightened. "But at least, if you decide not to listen to my request, will you let me know in advance? Especially if you decide to tell Myrtle?"

I hesitated, barely. "Of course."

Leo cast a surprised glance at me, but I ignored it. I was lying. If for some reason I felt I needed to tell Myrtle, there was no way I would tell Silas first. I could explain that to Leo in the Jeep, but it seemed the best course of action to placate Silas.

Silas took a sip of his wine, and then stood and dusted off his pants. "Thanks for listening to me. And, Fred, I meant what I said. If you need anything at all that can help you figure this out, let me know. Any sort of resources you might be lacking, I'll get for you. Whatever it takes to clear Myrtle's name."

"Thanks. And let me know if any more details come to you or things you think might help."

Watson had fallen asleep on the plush rug that sprawled between the couches, and he gave an annoyed groan as I woke him. Once more as we walked past the closet between the living room and the formal dining room, Watson whined and sniffed around the hardwood floor close to the doorway.

"I dropped a pan of prime rib the other night on the way back from the dining room. Apparently I didn't get it all cleaned up as well as I thought I did." Silas leaned down and ruffled Watson's fur, then glanced up at me. "I have a couple of scraps left over, if he'd like some. Seems mean to tempt him with such smells and leave him wanting."

"No, that's totally fine. But thank you. I appreciate it. He's had more than his share of calories today, trust me." I had to pull Watson's leash twice to get him to oblige, but with an irritated glare, he followed Leo and me out the door.

TWELVE

Branson was waiting for me as Watson and I pulled up to my cabin. And showing that he was every bit as stubborn and obstinate as I was, he hadn't taken shelter in his police cruiser, but sat on one of the log rocking chairs I'd gotten for my front porch, despite the cold. Or maybe, in spite of it.

Taking a moment to fasten the leash back onto Watson, I mentally told myself to stay calm, keep my temper in check, and play my cards close to the vest. No matter what Branson might say, I wasn't ready to share the information I learned from Silas simply to prove a point.

Watson growled as we approached the porch, and Branson stood, his tall, thick mass forming an imposing shadow. "Calm down, Watson. I love that you're protecting your mama, but I promise, she's always safe with me."

It had been a couple of months since he'd said something similar to Watson. It made me want to go back to that night. Although, I suppose we were about to. He'd arrived at my cabin to tell me to stay out of the case on that occasion as well. This time, though, I didn't think we were going to end up having grilled cheese sandwiches and chatting at my kitchen table.

As if proving my point, Branson's voice was cold when he spoke to me—not unfriendly necessarily, just distant. "Don't get all riled up, Fred. I'm not here to lecture. Although, would it have killed you to return even one of my calls or texts?"

"I didn't check them. So technically, I couldn't return them." I managed to make my tone less irritated than I felt.

To my surprise, he chuckled. "An attempt to ask forgiveness instead of permission?"

I shrugged as I unlocked the door. "You already denied your permission, and if you recall, I didn't ask for it." I opened the door and unhooked Watson's leash, and he scampered in from the cold.

"Don't worry, Fred. I'm not inviting myself inside. It's clear you would rather me not be here." Branson took a couple of steps across the porch, then stopped an arm's length away. I could swear he almost sounded hurt by the fact.

That annoyed me, and I turned on him. "Can you blame me? When I was looking into things about Declan's murder at Christmas, you gave me your full support. Even seemed impressed with what I was able to do, but on this one, you're acting like I'll mess everything up."

"I know that you realize I'm a police officer, Fred. Technically I'm not supposed to share any information with civilians or let them investigate. Even if I want to."

"Yes, of course I know that. But I don't care." I leveled my gaze on him. The night was bright, but under the porch eaves, we were in shadow. "Your department keeps messing it up. Again. Myrtle didn't kill Henry. I don't have proof of that, not yet, but I will."

He chuckled, and I nearly bit his head off, but he saved himself by speaking quicker than I could voice my temper aloud. "That's why I called. If you'd checked your messages. It wasn't Myrtle."

And that dumped an avalanche of snow on the fire of my fury. "What?"

He stepped a little closer still, his smile softening. "Despite the pin, Myrtle wasn't the killer. We have someone else in custody."

"Who?"

He sighed. "Fred, you know I can't...." Another laugh. "Oh, who am I kidding? Paulie Mertz."

I took a step back. "Paulie Mertz? That doesn't make any sense." Though I remembered he was one of two people on Silas's list.

"Now, please don't claim we've got the wrong person again." He raised a hand. "Let me save you the trouble of telling me that you have some sixth sense about this. I can promise you. We got our guy this time. We received an anonymous call that Paulie had illegal birds in his possession, and sure enough, he did, in the back room of his pet shop. It seems Henry had been threatening to expose him. So not only did we find the killer, we found our poacher. That should make Leo happy." There was accusation in that last line. But it was gone in an instant. "That's all I wanted to tell you, Fred."

I couldn't find words. Both for Branson once more giving me details of the case and because this wasn't right. Just like with Myrtle, I knew Paulie hadn't done this. Paulie was an example of when my gut had been wrong. Like everyone else, he'd struck me as rather strange and creepy, and desperate to an uncomfortable level. But he helped me when Watson had gotten into something dangerous right before Christmas, and I thought I'd seen past the hurting and desperate man who came across so off-putting. I even thought I might start to like him.

Branson stiffened. "Well, I guess that's all I wanted to say. Clearly you're not ready to move on, and I don't blame you." He truly did sound rather hurt. "I am sorry, Fred. I hope we can repair things." He gave a little nod and then walked off the porch and toward his car.

Another thought hit me, and I called out to him. "Wait."

He looked back hopefully.

"What about Paulie's dogs? Flotsam and Jetsam? Do you need someone to take care of them?" Paulie had two corgis, two hyperactive corgis that Watson would most definitely never forgive me if I allowed to come into our house, let alone stay for a while.

Branson's shoulders slumped slightly. "No. They're fine. The veterinarian, Dr. Sallee, is taking care of them." With another nod and a small wave, Branson disappeared into his car and drove off into the night.

"I can't believe you spent all morning baking, the rest of the day with customers, and then come home and bake for yourself?" I stared at the mess strewn over Katie's kitchen counter. She seemed much more haphazard when baking at home. "You're a sick, sick woman, Katie Pizzolato."

"And don't I know it!" Katie tore off a bit of sliced ham, and for the twentieth time in the past half an hour, tossed it to Watson, who was waiting aggressively at her feet. "As soon as you called asking to spend the night, I had to bake. We're having a slumber party. We need snacks."

"Snacks would be popcorn and M&M's, something easy, not your ham-and-cheese croissants."

Katie grimaced. "If you're going to consume that amount of butter and sugar, you might as well make it worth the calories." She tore off a bit of sliced cheese and popped it into her mouth. Watson whined in disappointment below her. "Sorry, buddy. I'm not completely selfless. I need some too." As she layered the ham and cheese and rolled the croissants, she cast more serious glances in my direction. "I'm glad you thought to give me a call, Fred. I imagine you're right. I doubt Silas had any ill intentions against you, but it's unsettling with him knowing where you live."

I made it about fifteen minutes after Branson left. I'd already changed into my pajamas and had a kettle of tea on the stove, ready to settle down in front of the fire and read, when Silas's voice on the phone telling me he knew where I lived crept in. The way he'd said it hadn't sounded threatening in the slightest. But in the middle of a dark woods, as the night grew deeper, and after multiple murders in such a short time, I wasn't sure if it was my gut speaking to me, or simply irrational fear, but I decided to go with it and called Katie.

"I'm probably being silly. Plus, according to Branson, it's all over. They caught the poacher and murderer all in one fell swoop."

Moving on to her next croissant, Katie *tsked*. "Please. You don't believe that any more than I do. Paulie's a strange little man, and rather uncomfortable to be around, but he didn't do this."

I agreed, but I was a little desperate for confirmation. "How do you know?"

"I have no idea." Katie shrugged, completely unconcerned. "I just do. So do you."

That I did. And maybe that was part of why I'd come to Katie's. For some reason, it seemed a little more dangerous, or something, to have the wrong person in jail for murder as opposed to no one. "Who do you think the murderer is?"

Katie didn't look up at me that time, keeping all her attention focused on the pastry. "I don't know. It sounds like you believe Silas loves Myrtle. And all his actions seem to make sense through that filter. I still don't think Myrtle did it, but I don't know. It sounded like Owen kind of gave you the creeps when you overheard him on the phone at the coffee shop this morning."

"He did. That's true. However, I was also completely flustered from making a fool of myself in front of Carla, but there was definitely something there. Though we've heard barely any rumors about Owen. Lots of cheating from Alice and Silas, but nothing about Owen."

Katie looked at me seriously. "Unless you take Henry at face value. Wasn't Owen the one he was saying was the poacher? He told Leo he had proof this time."

"I thought of that. Could simply be bad timing. To be accused of poaching and then Henry gets killed. Or it could be something more. Henry finally found the real poacher and paid the price." It made sense, and it didn't feel wrong either. But neither did it necessarily feel right. "Maybe I should go talk to

Owen tomorrow. Although, I don't know anything about him. It's not like he owns a store."

Katie stilled. "If you find him, I want you to take me with you. Or Leo, or Branson, even Sammy. Somebody. With all the names flying around, and the wrong people getting arrested, something about this feels a little more dangerous this time."

"More dangerous? You were the one who stopped an attempted murder a few weeks ago. *This* feels more dangerous?"

Katie considered, shrugged, and returned to the pastry. "Yeah, it does."

We continued tossing ideas back and forth, though none felt substantial, and ended up talking about Sammy as Katie debated whether she should bring her on full-time or if things would slow down at the bakery after the newness wore off. Soon the heavenly smell of butter, cheese, and bread filled the kitchen. It was almost as comforting as a good book.

As Katie took the croissants out of the oven to cool, she grinned over at me. "All right, go get into your pajamas, and I'll put on mine. You can't have a slumber party in real clothes."

"You're serious? A slumber party? Don't you have to be up at the crack of dawn to be at the bakery?"

Katie grimaced at the thought. "Spoilsport. Well, whatever. I want a slumber party. I was thinking of having a Harry Potter movie marathon, but maybe instead we should settle for an episode of something on Netflix. I suppose we should get *some* sleep."

"That does sound fun, how about—"

She held up her hand, cutting me off. "No, no murder mysteries. We get enough of that in real life. Try again."

"But I was thinking—"

"Nope." She smiled but narrowed her eyes at me. "You're cut off. No more thinking about murder, either in Estes or any other place on the television. I made the food; I'll pick the show." She headed toward the bedroom to change into her pajamas as she called out over her shoulder, "Oh, I know! We can watch *The Great British Bake Off*."

Not a bad choice. I liked that show, but I couldn't let Katie get the last word. "Seriously? I talk too much about murders, but you're allowed to dive into more baking?"

She didn't even bother to pop her head out of the bedroom door. "My house, my rules. Now shut up and get in your pajamas. I wish we had a pair for Watson."

Katie and I ended up watching three episodes of the baking show. And at nearly an hour a piece, we were up well past midnight. Though I slept on her couch, I didn't even hear her get up and head off to the bakery. When I finally woke at seven, she was gone, probably for hours and hours. I had no idea how she did it. Although I'd forgotten the luxury of having a doggy door and a dog run for Watson. He'd woken me three times during the night. Two of which were nothing more than him wanting to leave the house. As a result, I was dragging.

Once home, I made breakfast for Watson and myself, then got ready for the day. After a shower and half a pot of coffee, I almost felt human again. When I got to the bookshop, I'd go upstairs and get a dirty chai and whatever Katie had baked fresh that morning.

It had been a rough couple of days. I deserved a second breakfast.

Knowing full well how it would end, I drove past the Cozy Corgi, and on to the next block, to see if Myrtle was in. Nothing more. Simply to check.

Right.

There were some stores closed for the season, but the ones that weren't were already open, including Wings of the Rockies. It was still early enough that there was plenty of parking, so I pulled my Mini Cooper into a spot across the street, attached Watson's leash, and hopped out.

As I crossed toward her store, I realized I should be acting like a business owner. I wasn't a detective. I owned a bookshop. And currently there were at least one or two bakers in the upstairs of that bookshop and absolutely no one where the books were. I needed to hire someone.

I negated that thought as I opened the doors to Myrtle's store and allowed Watson to walk in ahead of me. There was no reason to hire someone—I wasn't always going to be solving a murder. This would be the last one. How many people could die in Estes Park, anyway? At least of murder.

Myrtle was on a ladder, affixing a copper bird-feeder to one of the ceiling beams. She looked even more like a crane than normal. "Fred. I figured I'd be seeing you today." She unwound a wire and slid the birdfeeder free. Taking it down, apparently, not putting it up. Twisting slightly, she bent and dangled the birdfeeder from the ladder. "Would you mind getting this for me? As soon as I got up here, I realized it wasn't one of my smartest ideas. But I was already up."

"Of course!" I dropped Watson's leash and hurried to her, reached up, and took the birdfeeder. It was heavier than it appeared.

Myrtle made her way down the steps. She seemed a little shaky. After she reached the bottom, she held out her hands for the birdfeeder. "Thank you."

I sucked in a gasp as Myrtle's eyes met mine. She'd aged a decade.

A blush rose to her thin cheeks. "And I thought maybe the mirror was lying. Guess not."

I considered telling her she looked fine. But she'd already read my face, and she'd looked in the mirror. The damage was done. "Are you okay?"

Myrtle laughed weakly and walked to the counter to set the birdfeeder down. She turned back to me, raking her fingers through her silver hair. Instead of its normal product-induced spike, it was a short fuzzy mess. Her eyes were bloodshot and red-rimmed, with painfully heavy bags. And still she trembled. "One of my brigade was murdered, I was taken in for that murder, and now another member of my brigade has been arrested. One who I don't think committed the murder." Her bottom lip quivered. "Which means one of my Feathered Friends is not only a murderer, but is free and willing to let someone else take the fall."

It wasn't the reaction I'd expected. I'd anticipated anger or at least irritation when she saw me. I reached for her arm, but stopped short of touching her, letting my hand fall back to my side. "I'm sorry that my turning in the pin caused you problems. Katie said that it wasn't even yours."

She shrugged like it didn't matter and leaned against the counter. "I don't blame you for that. It was the right thing to do. If the police had done their job better, they would've found the pin. Although, I do know there was a lot of snow up there. So either way, whether by their hand or yours, I would've been the natural suspect."

The door chimed, and an older man began to walk into the shop.

Myrtle closed her eyes as if trying to find strength, then leaned around a display of field guides and shook her head. "No, sorry. Not today. At least not right now. You should go shopping somewhere else."

He flinched. "But I—"

"I said no!" Myrtle let out one of her signature squawks, but this one was filled with panic and exhaustion.

I went over to the man, took him gently by the shoulder, and led him out the door. "Go to the Cozy Corgi. Tell the baker that Fred is giving you a pastry on the house."

He scrunched up his nose. "Who's Fred?"

Must not be a local. "I'm Fred."

"A woman named Fred." His nose became even more scrunched. "Well, Fred, I don't need a pastry. I'm needing some birdseed for—"

"She said no. I'm sorry." And she was probably getting ready to tell me the same thing the longer I took with the man.

"Well, of all the—"

He sounded like he was going to launch into a diatribe, so I stepped back into the shop, but couldn't bite my tongue fast enough before shutting the door. "On second thought, don't go to the Cozy Corgi. Go to the Black Bear Roaster instead. Try one of their scones." I shut the door and locked it.

"I didn't think I liked you when I first met you." Myrtle gave a quavering smile, and there was a hint of laughter in her voice. "But I've had Black Bear Roaster's scones. They're awful. You might be okay." A hiccup of a laugh exploded, then a real one, and then she burst into tears and sank to the floor.

"Oh, Myrtle." I rushed to her and attempted to put my arm around her, but she shrank away. I sat close, helpless, and had no idea what to do.

Watson padded over, his leash dragging behind him. He nudged his cold, wet nose against her hand, like he did with me when he determined I wasn't giving him enough attention.

I started to shoo him away, afraid what Myrtle's reaction would be. Afraid she might even swat at him. To my shock, still crying, Myrtle moved the hand he'd nudged to his head, and after a moment, her other began to slowly stroke his side. Watson pressed up against her thigh and rested there, allowing himself to be stroked.

Watson had come to me from out of nowhere. It was the fifth anniversary of my father's death, and I was sobbing at his gravestone, alone. And then Watson was there, curled up at my side, and he sat with me until the tears dried. When I got up to leave and he followed, I'd almost been surprised that he was real.

I put up flyers and announcements online about a lost dog. No one ever responded. I decided he'd been a gift from my father. Something to help me in my grief. It had been five years and many days my grief seemed as bad as the first. After Watson, things got better.

Watching Myrtle continue to stroke Watson, I was both touched by his atypical compassion and experienced a bite of fear. That somehow, when I got up to leave the store, Watson wouldn't follow, wouldn't want to go. That maybe he wasn't a corgi at all, but some chubby, furry, short-legged angel that stayed with people as they were hurting but then moved on when they were better.

Ridiculous.

But as Myrtle's tears began to dry, I couldn't keep that worry at bay.

After a few more minutes, Myrtle sniffed, reached above her to retrieve her peacock-feathered purse, and pulled out a tissue. Then she gave several honks as she blew her nose. She sighed a shaky exhale and patted Watson's head before looking over at me. "Good dog you got here. I'm more of a bird person myself, in case you didn't know." Though wavering, her smile was brighter that time. "But he's a good dog." She gave another pat and pulled her hand away.

Without hesitation, Watson stood, trotted around her outstretched legs, and took his place beside me.

I looked into his brown eyes. *You know, don't you? Both what I was worrying about and what I need right now.*

Watson let out a long sigh, one that almost seemed annoyed, then stretched out by my legs and plopped his head in my lap.

I felt my eyes sting in gratitude, and I stroked his bristly orange-and-white fur.

"Sorry about that. I feel like a fool." This time Myrtle's smile was simply embarrassed.

While refusing to break physical contact with Watson, I refocused on Myrtle. "No reason to be sorry."

"You believe that I didn't do it, don't you?"

"I do." I nodded and chuckled. "Of course, that doesn't mean that you didn't, but I don't think you did."

She nearly laughed. "Yeah, you're a little annoying, but I like you. I like you." She patted my leg, and to my surprise, made no move to get up, leaned back against the counter and seemed to deflate impossibly more. Though the tears appeared gone. "I have made a mess of things, Fred. I thought I was doing right. I really did."

I hesitated, almost wondering if she was about to make a confession, but I didn't think that was what she meant. "How so?"

She blinked several times. It didn't look like she was going to answer, but then she took a deep breath and launched in. "I don't like people very much. But I understand them, part of why I don't like them. I was looking for a way to do as much good as I could for the birds. I couldn't do it on my own. So I made the club. Twelve spots, because people like things that are exclusive. I made it expensive, ridiculously so, because people like things that are expensive. If I'd made it only a thousand dollar annual fee, people would've balked, but ten grand?" She laughed and winked at me. "Ten grand means it's expensive and doubly exclusive. And that's one hundred and twenty thousand a year that I can use to help save birds." Another laugh. "You know one way people are like birds?"

I felt like I was talking to a bird in human form every time I spoke to Myrtle Bantam. I figured it best not to say that. Though she'd probably take it as the highest form of compliment, come to think of it. "I can't say that I do."

"They are like starlings. Starlings love to steal and collect things. Fill their nests with worthless shiny trinkets." She tapped the badges on her chest. "I have twelve starlings who pay a lot of money to be special. Even if they have to cheat to make themselves feel that way."

I supposed it was a confession of sorts. "So you did know there was cheating."

"Of course I did. Don't you remember, I said I understand people. Why I don't like them overly much. But"—this time when she tapped her chest, I got the sensation that she was pointing deeper, past the badges—"that proves I'm human too, doesn't it? That I know about the cheating, and that I honestly don't care. Like the club matters, outside of raising awareness and making money to protect as many birds as I can. To me, the ends justify the means. So what if Alice has her son make bird sounds? Big deal if I've caught Roxanne sneaking a peek at my notes for the meeting beforehand and getting her trivia answers? It's a couple of people cheating. Maybe there is more that happens. The only two I'm sure of are Silas and Carl."

I wondered if Silas possibly had a more special

place in Myrtle's heart because of that belief or not. And I also wondered if it made me guilty that I knew the truth and wasn't planning on telling her.

She didn't give me the chance anyway. Myrtle grasped my knee, startling Watson, but he placed his head back in my lap. "See what I mean? I've created a club, filled it with people who are willing to pay to feel special, to cheat to feel special. I let it keep going, because the ends justify the means. So maybe"—tears brimmed in her eyes once more, but they didn't fall—"maybe that makes me responsible for Henry's murder, even though I wasn't the one who committed it."

I shook my head. "No. I don't believe that. Not for a second."

She scowled.

"I mean it, Myrtle. Sure, maybe there're some things that aren't exactly on the up and up about your club, but your reasoning makes sense. And even if those badges and the drive to feel special cause a few people to cheat, that's a far cry from murder."

Myrtle licked her lips and nodded slowly, like she wanted to believe it.

I wasn't sure how long her openness would last. Maybe she had decided she liked me, but as she said, she clearly wasn't a people person. Just because she wasn't going to call the cops on me every time I walked into her store, didn't mean she was suddenly going to be a bosom buddy. I needed to use the moment while I had it. Myrtle wasn't the only one who sometimes believed the ends justified the means. And if taking advantage of Myrtle's atypical openness helped free Paulie and led me to the true murderer, that was more than worth it.

I waited till her eyes met mine. "You don't believe Paulie killed Henry?"

"No." She sneered. "He's a little chick rushing around at the feet of all the other chickens in the barnyard, simultaneously trying to get their attention while hoping not to get stepped on. He didn't kill Henry or anyone else." She cocked her brow. "He also doesn't have poached birds in his store. Maybe he didn't know they were there or simply didn't know they were poached illegally. Paulie is one of the ones not here for his love of birds. Though he likes them well enough. He needed friends and is willing to pay for them. He's hardly the only one. Not everyone is here for the birds. Pete is looking for time away from his wife and kids, and a bird club is one of the few things his wife will allow him to do on his own. Benjamin's trying to sell cameras. Alice is attempting to fill the void her son left when he went to college. Roxanne likes to feel superior and special. Raul is the same as Pete. And Lucy... well, Lord knows why Lucy does anything." Myrtle shook her head, and sadness seemed to overpower her guilt and worry for the first time. "So you see, Henry was one of the very few who truly cared about the birds. Now the bird club is outnumbered by people who are here for other reasons. I've only got Silas, Petra, Carl, and Owen."

I latched on to Owen's name. "Really? You believe that Owen is truly here for the birds?"

Myrtle gave me a rather shocked expression. "Why? What have you uncovered? I don't know if I can take much more."

"Nothing." I debated how much to say but decided I might as well be direct. "Honestly, I don't know anything about Owen. But he was the last one Henry accused of being a poacher."

She rolled her eyes. "I love that Henry was dedicated to the birds, but he was an idiot. He accused everyone of everything. He was right about some of them, obviously. But more often than not, he was wrong. Owen was simply the latest person to be accused." She shook her head again. "Owen wouldn't be involved in poaching. He has only two badges, because of all of them, he does the one thing that matters. He pays *twenty* thousand a year to be in the club, simply to help the birds. More than anyone, he's here for that. And he's responsible for updating the computer system and putting in information when we spot rare birds and documenting when we notice things that are strange in the park." She narrowed her eyes as she thought. "Honestly, at times he makes me uncomfortable, but the same could be true for me. A lot of us in the club are rather... different. I can't say that Owen would or wouldn't be capable of murder. But he wouldn't be involved in poaching. The birds are much too important to him. He simply wouldn't do it. He was used to Henry's accusations. We all were. So even if I'm not sure if Owen could kill someone, there was no reason for him to kill Henry just because he was being accused of being the poacher once more. Nearly everyone had been accused at least three or four times of being a poacher by Henry, Owen included." She took a deep breath, and I could see Myrtle begin to come back to herself, growing both stronger and distant once more. "I have no idea why Henry was killed. But it wasn't because he accused one of the other members of cheating or being a poacher. I can promise you that."

The miracle of miracles happened after I spoke to Myrtle. Watson and I returned to the Cozy Corgi, and both of us did our jobs. I sold books, and Watson allowed a select few to pet him and then napped at his favorite spots in the sunshine.

Oh, and I had a second breakfast. A tart covered in blackberries and cherries. While Katie's baked goods were so far ahead of those offered at Black Bear Roaster they might as well have been different classifications of food entirely, she hadn't gotten the knack of the cappuccino and coffee machines quite yet. Her dirty chai had a lot to be desired. I discovered, on the other hand, that Sammy did have the knack. I'd been considering returning to the Black Bear Roaster simply for caffeinated beverages, if for no other reason than to attempt to maintain an amicable relationship with Carla. After tasting

Sammy's dirty chai, however, I decided I could wait for another day. Then I remembered how intensely awkward our last conversation had been. Maybe waiting for more than another day would be prudent.

By one in the afternoon, I was relieved of having to act like a responsible adult, as winter descended on the town once more and the customers stopped showing up. Katie and Sammy used the time to get a jump on the following day's prep work, and I opted to read.

I settled in with my book on the sofa, the warmth of the fire on one side, the light from the dusty-purple fabric of the Victorian Portobello lampshade above me, and the glow of snow flurries out the front window creating such a cozy environment, a person would think that murder could never happen within a hundred miles. And with the spicy aroma from Sammy's dirty chai wafting around me, I decided I was in heaven. The sensation was doubled when Watson let out a long yawn from his nap, stretched his little legs in front while his nearly tailless rump arched in the air, then he padded to the main room, through the fantasy and science fiction room in between, curled up at my feet by the fire, and fell asleep again.

As I read, following as Miss Fisher solved the

murder with more panache than I possessed, the details of Henry's death whirled around in my mind. That was just it, actually. I didn't have any details about Henry's death. His throat had been slit on a snowy night in the woods, surrounded by fourteen other people—most of whom he'd accused of multiple crimes and driven crazy. As far as hard evidence went, I had none, save for the kakapo pin. The only thing I knew for sure was that neither Katie, Leo, nor I had killed Henry. Nor the small herd of elk we'd been mesmerized by. Other than that, it didn't seem as if anyone had an actual alibi for the moment he'd been murdered. The ones who did, weren't trustworthy. I added Carl to the list; I did trust Carl. Which meant Roxanne was cleared as well. And my gut told me that Myrtle was innocent, as well as Paulie. But that was it. Everything else was a convoluted mess.

No wonder Branson told me to keep my nose out of it. Although, they weren't doing much better than me. They had brought in two different people for the murder, neither of whom had killed anyone. If my instincts were correct.

No sooner had I doubled down my effort to concentrate on the book, the front door of the shop opened, and I turned to see a tall figure bundled in a fur-lined parka.

He pulled his hood back as he searched the store, and then he found me. Benjamin.

I started to get up, but he motioned for me to stay as he hurried through the rooms toward me. As he walked, he slid off his parka and then joined me on the sofa. A few clumps of snow fell onto the fabric. I tried not to think about that. Gary and Percival had just refinished it. Hopefully snow wouldn't do any damage, but I was the one who put it in the shop. It would hardly be the last time snow got on it.

Watson shifted as Benjamin sat down, but simply repositioned and fell back to sleep.

As Benjamin turned his wide eyes to me, once again I realized how young he truly was—twenty-five at the absolute oldest, but probably a few years younger. Rather impressive that he owned his own camera shop at that age, come to think of it. I wondered what his story was. "You're dating Sergeant Wexler, right?"

I balked a little and sat straighter. I hadn't antici-pated that question. "No. I don't think I am."

Those wide eyes narrowed slightly. "You're not sure?"

I considered that for a heartbeat. "No, I'm not,

which probably means that I'm not dating Sergeant Wexler." I attempted a smile. "Wouldn't you say?" At the admission I felt a tingle of disappointment, or loss, some sense of unpleasantness I couldn't quite label. A bit of relief, too.

"Oh." Benjamin's expression fell. "Okay then. I thought you two were close." It looked like he was about to leave.

"Why do you ask? It seems like you were hoping Sergeant Wexler and I were dating for some reason?"

His fingers drummed quietly as he clutched the fabric of his coat. "It would've been good to have an in with someone at the police station." He seemed to consider, glanced at me, and apparently didn't find what he was looking for as he shook his head. "This was a mistake. Sorry. I'll let you get back to your book."

I grabbed his arm without thinking. "We've been on a couple of dates. And...." Good Lord, I couldn't believe what I was about to say. But I needed to know why Benjamin was here, and like Myrtle and I had spoken about that morning, the ends can sometimes justify the means. "He was at my house last night. We talked for a while. We might not be dating necessarily, but I think we're... something."

He searched my face again. "You think he'd

listen to you, like if you thought someone deserved a break, maybe he'd take your word on it?"

I thought that depended on the day. There were times I felt nearly certain he would, though none of those days had been lately. But still, I focused on those positive occasions as I answered. "Yes, I do. He did when Katie was accused of trying to kill Declan." At least that much was true, mostly.

Benjamin nodded slowly but was still perched on the edge of the sofa, ready to flee.

"Fill me in, Benjamin." While the stern professor routine had worked on him before, it seemed the young man now needed more of a motherly tone. Not an angle I had a lot of practice at. "It's clear something is eating you up. Obviously you know the right thing to do is to say whatever it is, or you wouldn't be here. If you're worried about Branson getting involved, I promise you I'll put in a good word."

"Okay." He still teetered on the edge of the sofa, but he nodded slowly. "I know Paulie didn't have anything to do with the poached birds. He didn't even know they were there."

While not exactly a revelation, I felt a sense of relief and vindication that my gut had been right. Mine, Myrtle's, and Katie's. "You do?"

Benjamin nodded and sighed in frustration. "I don't like the guy. But he doesn't deserve this. He's enough of a mess the way it is."

Suddenly I remembered who I was talking to, and I allowed some of that authoritarian professor past to slip back into my tone. "Is someone paying you to do this? Like they did with Myrtle?"

He snorted, then laughed. "For Paulie? Who would do that?"

He had a point.

"No, no one is paying me. In fact...." Benjamin twisted and glanced out the windows, then seemed satisfied and turned back around. "Me saying this is going to ruin a lot of things. A lot."

"You know who killed Henry?" The words slipped out before they'd even fully formed in my mind.

"No." Benjamin looked insulted. "Of course not. I told you before, I wouldn't cover for a murderer."

"Sorry." I brought what I hoped was a motherly tone back into my voice. "Then what's going on? How do you know Paulie didn't have anything to do with the birds?"

"Because, even though I don't know who killed Henry, I do know who's doing the poaching. At least, I think."

"You *think* you know who's poaching?"

He nodded and glanced at the windows once more.

He might honestly think he didn't know who the murderer was, but Benjamin was obviously scared. Which to me, meant he probably did know who the killer was, even if he didn't quite realize it. I reached out again and lightly touched his knee, bringing his attention back. "Who do you think is doing it, Benjamin?"

Once more, he studied me for a long time, clearly debating. From how serious he was taking it—he looked like he was debating jumping off a cliff—he must be fairly certain. He let out a long, heavy sigh. "Owen. I think. I only know of one illegal bird he's been involved with, but maybe he's done more."

Owen. The name was almost like a relief, after the way he'd looked at me when I overheard him on the phone the day before. Then I remembered Myrtle's claim about him a few hours ago. The one person in the group who paid double the membership fees to help the birds. "Are you sure? Myrtle thinks he's trustworthy."

"Like I said, I don't know if he's *the* poacher, the one the entire bird club seems obsessed with. He might not be, but I know he's done it once. And given what Silas asked me to do for Myrtle, I'm betting this is connected. No way Paulie has the backbone to be involved in poaching. The man jumps at his own shadow."

I agreed with Benjamin's assessment, but it still didn't make sense. "Why don't you tell me what you know? The whole story."

This time, he didn't hesitate before he began to talk; apparently having made up his mind, it was final. "I was paired up with Petra on the hike the other night, not for any real reason other than how it worked out. While we were in the woods, we ran across Owen. Petra pulled Owen off to the side but wasn't as quiet as she thought she was. She was mad, telling him that the bird he'd gotten her was sick. That she hadn't paid good money for a sick bird. She was starting to lose her temper, but Owen told her to be quiet and they'd discuss it later."

I replayed his story, trying to put the pieces together and needing more details. "Did Petra actually say that Owen procured an illegal bird for her, or simply that she bought a bird from him?"

Benjamin looked at me like I was daft. "Owen doesn't run a pet store. Why would he be selling a bird to Petra?"

Fair question, but it still didn't necessarily mean

it was poaching or even that the bird was illegal. "What does Owen do?"

He shrugged. "No idea."

"Did anything else happen? Are there any other details, even if you think they're not important?"

"I don't think so. Petra was definitely mad as we walked away, but she wouldn't talk about it. Not that I asked any questions. Wasn't much longer before Alice screamed and everybody came running."

One more bit of proof, however thin it was, that Henry had been right about Owen.

Maybe Henry had been nearby during the exchange, had heard, then confronted Owen about it.

"Doesn't necessarily clear Paulie, but maybe it gives enough reasonable doubt." I slipped back into professor mode once more. "You definitely should tell the police this. Maybe if they know it's Owen who they're looking for, that will help prove Paulie had nothing to do with it."

"I know. That's why I want you. Chances are, somehow, it'll come out that I lied about Myrtle. I need you to have my defense with Sergeant Wexler."

Maybe if I handed it directly over to him and didn't try to get more details on my own, Branson would listen to me. Although, I wasn't sure how much I was willing to go to bat for Benjamin. I thought he was telling the truth, but the only thing my gut told me about the kid was that I couldn't fully trust him. "I'll do my best." I pulled out my cell before Benjamin could object and tapped Branson's name.

He didn't answer. I didn't want to leave a voice-mail in case that startled Benjamin. Instead I called the police station. A voice I didn't recognize answered and asked if I was in the state of emergency. "No, I have some information about some possible poaching going on. I'd like to speak to Sergeant Wexler, please."

Benjamin flinched, realizing that I was on the phone with the police station instead of directly to Branson, and I covered the mouthpiece of the phone to whisper to him. "It's fine. He wasn't answering his cell. It's still Branson. And if you bolt, it'll make you look guilty."

The dispatch put me through.

Branson answered on the second ring. "When they said you were calling, at first I thought it was because you'd forgiven me. But apparently you have information about a case?"

I was a little surprised he'd been worried about me being mad. But I didn't have time to focus on that. "Benjamin is with me at the bookshop. And no, I didn't go snooping this time. He's got a story for you about a possible poacher, one that may prove Paulie is innocent."

Branson hesitated, probably thrown off by me not responding to his question about forgiveness. "Benjamin has information about a poacher?" His voice was cold suddenly. Clearly hurt, or something, that I called him for professional reasons instead of personal.

"Yes."

"Okay, be right there."

It took nearly twice as long for Branson to get to the Cozy Corgi as I'd expected, and by the time the police cruiser pulled up in front of the shop, Benjamin was pacing the floor. To my surprise, Branson hadn't come alone. Officer Green came with him, and from both their expressions, it was clear they'd been arguing on the way over. Branson attempted a smile as they entered the shop, but it fell flat.

Susan glowered as he leaned close enough to me to not be overheard.

"Sorry. I was planning on talking to the two of you here, but Susan got wind of it and apparently we're going to do this by the book. She made a whole scene of it. Sometimes I'm not sure if I'm the superior officer or if she is." He turned to Benjamin. "You're not under arrest. I'm simply going to request you come with us to the station. You can even follow us in your own car if you'd rather. We'll take your official statement there."

Benjamin looked at me in a panic, then back at them. "Is Fred coming too?"

Susan snorted. "Is she involved in this case, or part of what you witnessed? Something more than simply being nosy, obviously."

He shook his head, and Susan grinned. Branson's features darkened.

I watched from the window with Watson at my feet as Benjamin got in his car and followed the police cruiser out of sight.

"Well, look who it is." Leo grinned as he opened his apartment door, and though his tone was teasing, his eyes had a flash of heat. "It's feast or famine with you, isn't it?"

Watson let out a happy yelp and reared upward, bashing his forepaws into Leo's knees.

As with every other interaction they'd had, Leo gave in to whatever Watson demanded, sinking down onto one knee and rubbing Watson nearly silly, like he was a joyful little puppy inside of the cantankerous old soul that he was.

Watson loved it.

I stepped around them and shut the door, glad to be out of the cold. "Thanks for letting me come over. I wasn't sure if you'd be available when I called."

"Today is one of my days off." He finished lavishing affection on Watson and stood. "You're always welcome, but you said you had news. Gotta say, I'm curious." He motioned toward the sofa where we'd sat before. I'd not even crossed the room before Watson raced past me and leaped onto the couch, automatically taking the center spot.

"Well, Watson feels at home." Leo sat down beside him, and instantly began stroking his fur as he waited for me to begin.

I sat and didn't waste any more time. "Benjamin came and saw me. And he left with the police probably less than half an hour ago."

Leo jerked, startling Watson. "Sorry, buddy." He started petting him again and refocused on me. "Benjamin? *Benjamin* killed Henry?"

"No. He wasn't arrested. He went in for questioning. He kinda volunteered. He thinks he knows who the poacher is."

This time Leo went stone-cold still.

A phone vibrated over on the kitchen counter. I motioned toward it. "You can get that if you want."

"Are you crazy? Like I care about the phone right now." Leo's eyes were wide, and he was pale suddenly. "I know there's more than one poacher, but we've not been able to pin anybody in forever. Who did he say?"

That was why I'd come to see Leo in person. I knew how big this was for him. And maybe some part of me was looking for an excuse to see him. Possibly, but I wasn't going to consider that aspect. "Owen."

"Owen?" A laugh burst from Leo, but it trailed off quickly, his expression growing serious once more. "You're serious?"

I nodded. "Yes. I called Myrtle before I came over here. She and I talked earlier in the day. She doesn't believe it. She thinks Benjamin's lying. Which, he seems prone to do."

Leo didn't speak for a little bit, and his gaze grew distant, but his fingers never quit dragging through Watson's fur, a pile beginning to grow in the crease of the couch cushions.

I started to ask if he was okay, then thought better of it.

"Owen. I never would've considered Owen. Nobody in the bird club would, except Henry, and he suspected everyone. Which, if Owen is the poacher, would've made things pretty easy on him." Though his eyes were narrowed, I could already see he was accepting the possibility. "What proof did Benjamin have?"

"Apparently Petra bought a bird from Owen,

and now the bird is sick. Benjamin heard them arguing about it the night of the snowshoe hike."

"Petra?" One of his hands left Watson and touched his heart. He looked wounded. "She's crazy about birds. I can't believe she would do that." Leo shook his head and mumbled to himself. "I bet it's a forest owlet."

"A forest owlet?"

"Yeah, cute little thing from India. Critically endangered. She's nearly as obsessed with them as Myrtle is with the kakapo." Leo sank back into the cushions, finally breaking contact with Watson and looking utterly devastated. "Right in front of my eyes. This whole time. Right in front of my eyes."

"None of this is confirmed. I'm not telling you this so you'll beat yourself up." I reached over Watson and gripped Leo's forearm. "And even if it is true, you're not a member of the bird club. You're only there occasionally. You've got the entire national park to think about. Myrtle does this full-time, and she's as shocked as you are. The last we spoke, she didn't believe it. About Owen or Petra. She barely let me finish before she cut me off. I wanted you to know, but I also thought with the new information and you knowing the members of the Feathered Friends Brigade much better than I do, that maybe this news would trigger something for you. Can you see Owen as the poacher? And if so, as a killer? Or Petra?"

He laughed again. It burst from him in an almost crazed fashion. "Petra? Can *you* picture Petra murdering someone?"

The idea of the little Asian grandmother slitting a man's throat in the woods did seem a little farfetched, but you never knew. "She wouldn't be the first little old lady who's killed someone in the past couple of months."

Leo sobered. "Well, that's true. But no, I can't see Petra doing that. I also can't see her being a poacher. If she is involved, then maybe she's nothing more than a buyer. It happens sometimes. People love a certain animal so much that they can no longer love it from afar. They have to possess it."

"Sounds like a bad romance. At least a bad one-sided one."

"It's a pretty apt description." Leo shook his head again and sighed, sounding utterly defeated. Then he put his hands on his knees and shifted to a standing position. "I found the canister of pink-lemonade mix so I made a pitcher. Want a glass as we see if we can figure this out?"

I couldn't hold back a chuckle. "You know, that sounds pretty good."

Leo walked around the couch, through the small living room, and into the kitchen. I watched as he pulled the pitcher from the refrigerator and set it on the counter by his phone. He picked up his cell, his eyebrows creasing, then glanced my way. "I have a text from Myrtle."

I stood instantly and made my way over to him. No way was that a coincidence.

"Myrtle says she thinks she knows who the poacher is. She wants me to come to the shop and see what she's found." Without waiting for a response, he tapped the screen and lifted the phone to his ear. Several seconds passed before he lowered it. "She's not answering."

My skin prickled, but I ignored it. "She could be with a customer."

Leo glanced at his cell. "It's almost five. She could be." His honey-brown gaze lifted and met mine. A few more moments passed. "Should we go to her?"

"If you don't, I will."

Leo grinned.

The sun was setting by the time we parked in front of Wings of the Rockies. The snow was thicker than before, and the downtown was empty of people. Leo waited for Watson and me to exit the Jeep and then hit Lock. There was still an Open sign in the window, and the three of us walked in. The chimes chirped overhead like always, but the store was silent.

Watson growled in the back of his throat.

Leo and I looked at each other. My skin prickled once more.

"Myrtle?" Leo's loud voice caused Watson and me both to jump, and I instinctively threw out my arm, as if he was in the passenger seat and we were about to wreck.

I shook my head. Maybe I was being silly, but I could feel it. All three of us could. Something was clearly wrong.

We made our way through the store, glancing behind little nooks and crannies as we walked, and then behind the counter. There was nothing. No one.

I glanced at Leo. "Try calling her again."

He did. After a couple of silent seconds, we heard the sound of songbirds in the distance. Leo motioned toward the door in the back. "Over there. That's her ringtone."

We walked to the door, and I suddenly wished we'd brought a weapon of some sort.

Leo threw open the door and cursed. This time he held out his arm. "You don't need to see this."

I stepped past him and into a large room. Over half of it was simply storage and merchandise; the other side was a makeshift office. Desk, computer, shelves of books. In front of the desk, lying in a pool of blood on the floor was Owen. Like Henry in the forest, his eyes were sightless. I could see two knife wounds, and it was easy to tell which one had killed him.

Watson growled, but I didn't try to shush him.

Leo started to walk over to Owen's body.

"Leo, what are you doing?"

He paused and looked back. "I need to check and make sure he's not alive. Maybe he—"

"No, he's dead. Don't touch him. Don't check." I was surprised at the steel in my voice. It didn't quaver in the slightest. Although this was my fifth dead body in three months, and by that point, I should be perfectly clear I wasn't the fainting type. "It'll mess up the scene. And possibly get you brought in as a suspect."

For a second he looked like he was going to argue, but then he didn't. "No Myrtle."

I'd forgotten. "Call her cell again." No sooner were the words out of my mouth than I saw it. "No, never mind. It's on the desk." The phone was lying on a stack of papers, but Myrtle's peacock-feathered purse was on the ground, the contents strewn over the floor, beside a gun I'd not noticed before. "I don't think Myrtle did this, and I don't think she left willingly."

Leo followed my gaze and nodded. "Call the cops?"

"Yeah." I nodded. "I'll do it."

Branson answered. "Don't tell me you have another witness or person with information." He sounded stressed, but there was a slight playful teasing in his tone.

"A dead body, actually. At Wings of the Rockies."

There was a heartbeat. "Are you serious?"

"Unfortunately, yes."

"Myrtle?"

I shook my head again, then realized he couldn't see it. "No. Owen."

"Owen?" His voice shot up, clearly shocked.

"Yes. And I'm pretty certain Myrtle's been taken

against her will. At least her phone is here, and her purse is spilled all over the place."

"I'll be right there. And Fred?"

"Yeah?"

"Don't go anywhere, and don't touch anything." I could almost see him roll his eyes. "The last thing I want is to have to waste time trying to keep Susan from locking you up because your fingerprints are on something."

"Got it." I ended the call and looked at Leo. "They're on their way."

He grunted, but seemed unable to tear his eyes from Owen.

I grabbed his arm. "Come on. That doesn't mean we need to wait in here."

We started to leave the office, but Watson was stretched to the end of his leash, growling quietly at a file cabinet.

I started to call him and force him to come, then thought better of it. I spoke to Leo, though I didn't glance back at him. "Hold on." I walked over to Watson, and felt Leo behind my back as I knelt down.

Watson continued to growl.

Ridiculously, I feared he'd found Myrtle's body. Preposterous, since there wasn't room. At first I didn't see what had caught his attention, and I had to adjust my position to better see between a stack of boxes and the file cabinet, and then I saw the glint of silver. Carefully, I used the hem of my skirt as a glove and pulled it out.

"A knife." Leo put his hand on my shoulder.

A large knife. Obviously what had killed Owen, judging from the freshness of the blood on it. Though I couldn't imagine why it was there.

Leo sucked in a breath. "Fred, look." He leaned forward, pointing at the knife, but stopping short of touching it. "There's a kakapo inlaid on the handle." He pulled his hand back. "It must be Myrtle's."

I started to nod and then stopped. "No. It's not Myrtle's." I stood and looked Leo full in the face. "Though I bet I know where Myrtle is, or at least who she's with." This time I did have to pull Watson to get him to move and headed toward the door. I glanced back at Leo, who was fixated on Owen once more. "You coming with me?"

Despite his pale face, a flicker of a grin played at his lips. "You know it."

We were nearly across town when Branson called.

In the haste, I'd forgotten all about him and nearly hit Ignore. Then realized we were more than likely going to need the police for the upcoming situation. "Hey, sorry I—"

"Where are you?" He sounded furious. "I told you not to leave."

"I know who took Myrtle. Leo and I are headed to his house right now."

"You're what?" His voice rose nearly an octave, then crashed to a whisper. "You're with Leo?"

"Yes, the two of us were going to go talk to Myrtle, and that's when we discovered Owen's body."

Leo cast a sidelong glance at me, then refocused on the snowy road.

"Either way, I told you not to leave. And you have no business going on a rescue mission. I don't need you getting killed too."

"I won't." There wasn't time for this. "We're almost there, and I'm not stopping now. They might not even be here, but it's probably a good idea for you to head over." I filled him in on where we were headed. Branson sputtered indignantly the entire time.

We pulled into Silas's driveway, and Leo slammed the Jeep into Park. "All right, stay here. I'll be right back, hopefully."

I gaped at him. "What do you mean, stay right here?"

"If we're right, which I'm sure we are, Silas killed Owen less than half an hour ago. We don't need to add another victim."

He started to reach for the door handle, but I cut him off. "And what are you? Are you not a people— er person? Or does being a park ranger make you somehow invincible?"

"Fred." Unlike Branson, Leo's voice wasn't patient, just pleading. "I don't want you to get hurt."

"Well, good. That makes two of us. I don't want to be hurt either." I could feel my nostrils flare, and my temper began to take over. "Nor do I want you hurt. And chances are that both of us are less likely to get hurt if we go together."

For a second, I thought he was going to continue to argue, but then a grin began to form. "Fine. You're probably right. You can come."

Despite the fact we were more than likely sitting outside the home of a killer and getting ready to go confront him, I laughed. "Excuse me, did you just give me permission?"

"No, I was—" He blushed. "Sorry. Didn't mean to do it that way. I simply want you to be safe."

"We've covered that. Let's do our best to make sure the other stays safe, all right?" I glanced back at Watson. "I'll be right back."

We hurried up the sidewalk, got to the door, and I turned to Leo, unable to keep a smile from forming. "Okay, I didn't plan this part out. What do you think? Break a window, ring the doorbell, go around the house and look for unlocked doors?"

He considered for a second and then answered in a tone that was more of a question. "Ring the doorbell?"

"That's kinda what I was thinking." I pushed the

doorbell. "This is insane." Even so, I held up my hand to the etched glass oval on the front door and peered in. A large blurry form moved through my field of vision from farther back in the house, in the living room, if my memory served. "Ring the bell again, Leo."

He did.

The large form returned, silhouetted against the light of the room behind him. I was sure it was Silas, and he stiffened when he saw me pressed against the window. He dropped whatever he'd been carrying and pushed it to the side, then to my surprise, strode toward the door. I jerked back on instinct but then forced myself to look again, checking his hands. So many things I'd not considered. His hands were empty, and I pulled back once more.

"I don't think he's holding a gun, but that doesn't mean he doesn't have one somewhere nearby."

"I don't have a gun, but I do have a crowbar in the back of the Jeep."

I spared him a glance. "I don't think you have time to go get it, and it's probably best not to show up looking like we're ready to attack. For all he knows, we're here to talk about what we discussed before. Nothing else."

"Yeah." Leo sounded skeptical. "I don't think that's how this is going to go."

I didn't either.

But there was no more time to consider or predict. Silas opened the door, not wide but enough to make me wonder if maybe he wasn't sure why we were there. "Fred, Leo." He was wide-eyed and pale. Probably in shock. "Now is not a good time."

Even before I said it, I knew it was pointless. "I've given some thoughts to what you requested. About keeping your feelings about Myrtle secret from her. I talked to her this morning; she was a complete wreck. I think maybe hearing that someone loves her might help."

He laughed softly, a crazed smile forming on his lips. "She knows." He started to shut the door. "You should leave now."

I put my hand up to stop it, and Leo took a step closer. "That's not going to work, Silas." I decided to go with the direct approach again. It seemed more effective most of the time. "I want to see Myrtle. Have you hurt her?"

Silas flinched and relaxed his hold on the door, allowing me to nudge it open a little more. "I would never hurt Myrtle. Ever."

"What about Owen? Or Henry?"

Silas cast his wild eyes on Leo. Maybe that had been a little too direct. "I need you to leave, Leo." He straightened, squaring his shoulders, and his voice grew hard. "I don't want to hurt you. I like you." His gaze flicked to me. "Both of you. But I will hurt you, if you don't leave right now."

"Silas, we have to see Myrtle." I tried the same mothering tone I'd used on Benjamin. The aggression was growing thick and needed to be cut somehow. "I only want to know she's okay."

"I already told you, I would never hurt her." Silas started to slam the door, but Leo barged past, knocking me a little off-balance, and plowed into Silas.

I steadied myself on the wall of the porch, and watched as Leo and Silas were airborne in a weird embrace through the doorway, then crashed to the hardwood floor, causing the chandelier to shake and send a rainbow of fractals over the scene. Silas let out a cry as the back of his head hit the floor.

Leo repositioned quickly, straddling Silas and managing to secure both his wrists to the ground.

Silas began to buck.

Leo looked like he was bull riding for a moment,

then pressed harder on Silas's wrists and dug his knees into Silas's ribs. "Don't struggle, Silas. I don't want to hurt you either, so don't make me."

Silas stilled.

For just a heartbeat, I was so thrown off that I stared. I might've expected such a move from Branson, but not from Leo. From all our interactions, and Katie's constant reference to him as Smokey Bear, that was exactly how I'd begun to see him. Some big, softhearted teddy bear.

There was nothing reminiscent of a stuffed animal as he glanced over his shoulder. "I've got ropes in the Jeep. Get them, please."

I nodded and rushed toward the Jeep, slipping on a patch of ice on the walkway but catching myself easily. I almost laughed when I realized Leo had managed to say *please* as he pinned a murderer to the ground. The Jeep was unlocked, and I threw open the back door to find a huge assortment of equipment. The crowbar was there alongside an axe, and several coils of ropes. At least he was still teddy bear enough to not request the axe.

Watson peered over the back of the seat, whining pitifully.

"Sorry, buddy, be right back. Everything's okay."

I grabbed the ropes and hurried back to Leo, who still had Silas secured.

"Tie up his right wrist." Leo carefully slid his hands down Silas's forearm, making room.

I wedged the end of the rope under Silas's hand, and looped it, before starting the knot. I had a flash like an out-of-body experience as I worked. As if I was spying on us from the chandelier, I could see the three of us on the ground and marveled as I expediently tied rope around a man's wrist. Surely it should be disturbing that I didn't even hesitate.

From out of nowhere, Watson bounded through the door. He let out a ferocious bark, and as his hind foot caught on the doorjamb, he stumbled, plowing into Leo's side.

It wasn't much, but it was enough. Leo's grip on Silas loosened, and my hands were fixing the knot, leaving less pressure on the rest of his arm. As Silas swung a fist through the air, the rope slapped across my face, and his fist smashed into Leo's temple.

Though Leo let out a yell, he managed to hold on to Silas all the same, but Silas used the momentum of his swing to force a roll. He was unable to do it completely, and he and Leo ended up on their sides. With a startled yelp, Watson darted out of the way, then realized Leo was in trouble and rushed back in to bite Silas's ear, instantly drawing blood.

Silas howled and swung again, this time at Watson. Still having the rope in my hand that was secured to his wrist, I threw myself backward from my kneeling position yanking the rope as hard as I could.

There was a snap, and another yell.

"Freeze!"

I yanked harder at the rope, eliciting another scream from Silas.

"Fred! I said freeze."

I wasn't sure who I thought shouted the first *freeze*, but it startled me when I looked over to see Branson and Officer Green both pointing their guns at Silas.

I froze but didn't lessen my hold on the rope.

Watson growled, still tugging on Silas's ear.

"Fred. You can unfreeze enough to remind Watson he's a corgi not a German shepherd." There was a hint of laughter in Branson's tone.

I hesitated to release the rope, fearing Silas would take a swing at Watson, but then I noticed the unnatural angle of his arm. He wasn't going to be doing anything to Watson. I supposed I'd done that.

Releasing the rope, I slid an arm under Watson's belly and pulled him from Silas.

He snarled, then realized it was me and settled.

"Good boy," I whispered in his ear as I ruffled his fur. "You're my good, brave boy." I'd made plenty of jokes about Watson killing me in my sleep. I was going to have to reconsider those. I hadn't known he had it in him.

"You too, Lopez. Let him go. We've got it from here."

In a matter of minutes, Branson and Susan had Silas handcuffed and read him his rights. Susan kept her gun trained on him, even after he was hand-cuffed, which had sent Silas into fits of howling. She glanced at me occasionally, and I wondered if she was considering pointing the gun somewhere else.

Branson turned to us. "Myrtle?"

I shook my head. "As you can see, we didn't quite make it past the doorway."

He snickered. "I almost wish we'd been a couple of minutes later. Dislocated arm, chewed up ear... any longer and the guy might've been total dog food." He glanced around, his eyes wide as he took in the mansion. "If she's here, we've got a lot of rooms to search."

"No, I know where she is." I motioned toward

where Watson was sniffing in front of the door, the same one he'd smelled before. This time there was the key and the lock. "For some reason, I don't think that's a closet."

Branson headed over, twisted the door handle, and looked in, then let out a low whistle.

Watson rushed past him.

Leo and I both hurried to follow, and I could see the objection rising to Branson's lips as we neared the door.

"Sergeant Wexler." Susan's voice froze us in our places. "These are civilians. They need to stay here."

"You know, Susan." I didn't think I'd ever heard Branson's voice sound so cold. "It's time you remember that you're outranked." He stepped through the doorway, gun drawn, and gestured with his head for us to follow.

I gave a mental thanks to Susan, certain Branson was letting us follow simply because she'd told him he shouldn't.

The reason Branson had whistled was instantly clear the moment Leo and I looked in the doorway, and we turned to stare at each other before going in.

Indeed, it was not a closet, but a long set of stairs. But that was where the comparison to anything house-like stopped. Every step we took brought us into a new world. And with every one, we left the winter wonderland of Estes behind and entered a hot and humid rainforest.

The ceilings were at least twenty feet high, though maybe taller. It was hard to tell with the large growths of trees and vines covering the space. It looked like it went on forever. The ground was dirt, rock, moss, and different sorts of vegetation. A small stream babbled through the center. And sitting on its bank, looking completely dazed and in shock was Myrtle. Her hands and feet were bound, and there was a bruise forming on the side of her face, but other than that she looked no worse for the wear. Beside her, Watson pressed against her, barking at us like we couldn't see them. And above everything, were birds. Countless birds. Parrots of every color imaginable, finches, and doves, and all sorts of song-birds I didn't have the names for. And then I realized it wasn't only above us, but everywhere. Behind Myrtle and Watson, a peacock strode between the trees. All sorts of birds—some I recognized, others I didn't—wandered about, a few of them playing in the stream.

We were all rather shocked, and it took us several moments frozen at the base of the steps before we entered the world and rushed to Myrtle's side.

Ten minutes later, police were scouring the house, and Susan and another officer had taken Silas away.

We'd started to bring Myrtle up, but she begged to stay where she was. So after getting her a glass of water, Leo, Watson, and I sat on the bank of the indoor stream with her, while Branson paced, asking endless questions.

"You're certain Owen was the poacher?"

Myrtle nodded. She seemed more herself every second, and she didn't appear to be closing off like she normally did, though she never met any of our gazes. She was constantly looking everywhere, every once in a while gasping at the sight of a new bird she'd not noticed. "Yes. After I spoke to Fred this morning, I made a surprise visit to Petra. What Fred said was true. Petra admitted she'd got the bird from Owen."

"An owlet?"

Branson cast Leo an irritated glare for interrupting, but Myrtle answered him anyway.

"Yes. One that's not doing very well, I'm afraid." Her eyes tracked a red macaw that let out a screech and landed on a branch over our heads.

"And then I started checking the books. Owen helped me with a lot of the financial stuff for the club. Honestly, I'm not sure what it means, but something was wrong with the notes. I don't think money was missing, but there was also documentation of where we spotted rare birds nearby, which makes sense, but also some states over." She shrugged. "In and of itself, not a big deal, but considering what I'd seen at Petra's, it made me wonder."

"We'll need to take those books as evidence, Myrtle. More proof of what Owen was up to." Branson made a note in his pad.

"Maybe you can finally put a stop to the poaching ring that's been going on." Leo cast a hard stare at Branson. "It's not one person. Owen might be part of it, but he's merely a part. We've got a poaching ring going on in—"

"Don't get carried away, Leo." Before Leo could respond, Branson refocused on Myrtle. "What did Owen say to you?"

"I was at the shop with Silas. When I found the books, I called him to see what he thought." She finally looked away from the birds and glanced at Leo. But only for a second. "I texted you while Silas was there. I wanted your input as well. Silas was saying that I was reading into the books too much. That Owen wouldn't do such a thing." Her gaze grew distant, seeming not to focus even on the birds anymore, probably lost to the recent memory. "Then Owen showed up. He'd heard about Benjamin being taken in for questioning, and Petra had called him to let him know that I knew about the owl. He came there to kill me. He and Silas started arguing. Owen was saying that I knew too much, that I couldn't live. Silas kept telling him that I could be trusted and that we were going away soon anyway." She shivered. "Owen pulled a gun and was going to shoot me, but Silas... stopped him."

All of us were still.

"So that means Silas killed saving you." I took her by the hand, keeping my other on Watson. The last thing we needed was for him to decide to do a replay of a bird chase. "So he's not a murderer, at least not in that sense."

"Yes, he is." She turned sad eyes on me. "He killed Henry. That wasn't Owen."

"Why?" Leo sounded truly shocked.

She shivered again. "Because of how he spoke to me. The way Henry screamed at me that night in the woods. I was the reason. Silas told me like he thought I would thank him." She gestured around the rainforest. "He made this for me. So he said. A place for me to visit when I lived with him one day." She took a shaky breath, and I thought she was near tears, but none came. "All of these birds are poached, at least most of them, taken from their homes and brought here—no matter how beautiful it is, it's still a cage. *For me*. He committed this atrocity for me." She shrugged again. "I guess Owen did it, technically. He's the one who got the birds for Silas, but it was Silas's money that made it happen. For me. How could he ever think that I would want this?"

I squeezed her hand. "This isn't your fault."

She spared me a glance. "I don't know about that. Maybe if I'd paid more attention to the people around me. The ones I trusted the most are responsible for the very thing I hate. I had no idea Silas felt for me the way he did. Maybe if I'd realized, I could've ended it before his obsession grew."

"It's still not your fault, Myrtle." In a strange way, I could see, partly, why Silas would think Myrtle would like this place. If I didn't know the ugly part about the poaching, even I would've loved it, and I didn't have any great affinity for birds. They were fine, beautiful, but I was much more of a dog person. This was like stumbling upon a bit of magic. But for Myrtle, it was nothing more than a cage.

"I still don't understand why your pin was near where Henry was killed." Branson's voice wasn't necessarily hard, but it didn't seem like he fully trusted her yet.

"I've told you. It wasn't mine. It was Silas's."

He looked like he was about to argue, so I jumped in. "I think that's true. The knife we found, which we didn't touch, has a kakapo on it, just like the pin. I think because it was Myrtle's favorite bird, it became Silas's way of having her close."

"Silas told me that was his one mistake." She motioned toward the treetops. "If you look on the kitchen counter, you'll find two plane tickets. For ten months from now. Silas said he hoped I would fall in love with him within the year. He bought us plane tickets to New Zealand so I could finally see a kakapo. He said that since I knew early, he'd try to move up our reservations. And he had the pin made for me. He was going to give it to me there. He claimed he carried it with him everywhere."

Branson continued asking question after question. Still distrustful. But every answer she gave was solid.

Finally it was time to go. Myrtle stood with us and looked around. At last tears fell. "May I have a little time down here, by myself? I know they shouldn't be here, and I'm going to do everything I can to make sure every single one of them returns to where they came from, but I have never seen so many birds, so many different kinds of birds, in one place."

Branson started to shake his head, but I caught his eye. After a few seconds, he gave a nod. "Of course, Myrtle. We'll be upstairs. Join us whenever you're ready."

Snow fell through the night and continued into the next morning. I watched from the bakery window as large crystalline flakes floated over downtown. Estes truly was the most charming little town, if you overlooked the recent murders. Carl shuffled through the front door of Cabin and Hearth with a broom and dusted off the sidewalk in front of the store. I'd have to pop in at some point during the day and fill him and Anna in on all the details. Goodness knows they'd earned it. Maybe I'd invite my uncles down to do it all at once. In the distance, the sun shone brightly on the mountains, promising that the snow was short-lived.

"What I don't understand is how the two of you were in Silas's house and couldn't hear all those birds. My grandmother had a cockatoo when I went to live with her. That thing drove me absolutely crazy, all that screeching and squawking and hollering." Katie bugged her eyes. "And that was just one bird."

I came back to the moment, focusing on my friend and business partner. "You went to live with your grandma? How old were you?"

She stiffened slightly. "I don't know, twelve or something." She waved me off. "That's most definitely not interesting. Not near as interesting as a killer with a jungle in their basement."

I never pushed too far into Katie's past. She'd tell me one day when she was ready. I was certain there was something there. But if she was never ready, that was fine too.

Leo finished chewing a bite of his ham-and-cheese croissant before answering. "That room was basically a fortress of its own. Soundproofed, completely insulated. If nobody realized what was going on, Silas could've had Myrtle down there for the rest of her life, and no one would've ever known. There was no way she could've escaped. What we thought was a closet door was as thick as a vault. I can't imagine how much that place cost to build. Or to simply keep going. I'm surprised the energy company didn't raise a stink over the heating bill alone."

I bent down, reaching under the table to scratch Watson's head. "But you knew, didn't you? You smelled something. You knew there was something good in that room."

"I was thinking about that last night as I fell asleep." Leo glanced under the table as well, smiling at Watson before looking back at Katie and me. "As good as a dog's nose is, I can't imagine he would've been able to smell through that door. That seal was impermeable. My guess is he was smelling where Silas's shoes had been, or something—when he would walk up from the basement."

"Any of you want refills?" Sammy gestured at me as she walked up to our table. "I know you want another dirty chai. I think you have a drinking problem."

Katie swatted at her, shooing her away. "You were not hired to be a waitress. You're not getting paid enough to be a waitress. You're a baker."

Sammy chuckled but lifted her eyebrows in a questioning manner at me as she walked away so Katie couldn't see her.

I smiled and nodded. I could do with another dirty chai. Sammy seemed nearly as comfortable in her role of baker as Katie, almost like she felt a sense of ownership. I hoped that was a good thing.

Katie reached over and took a piece of my bear claw but spoke before she popped it in her mouth. "I feel horrible for Myrtle. To have members of her club be involved in that. I'm sure she's devastated. What's going to happen to Petra?"

"I'm not sure." Leo shrugged. "She's not in jail or anything, but purchasing a poached animal could come with jail time. My guess is she'll get a hefty fine."

I hadn't even thought of her that morning. I turned to him. "What about the owl... sorry, owlet?"

He grinned. "Dr. Sallee is keeping her for the time being. I'm betting he'll get her back into shape. The bigger issue is figuring out where all the other birds came from. And how long they've been gone. If it's safe to send them back, or if they've been too domesticated. Unfortunately, I figure most of them will end up in zoos. Which isn't necessarily a bad life, by any means. But—"

"Still a cage, as Myrtle would say." I hadn't meant to interrupt him, but the words that sprung from my lips brought a bit of melancholy. "That's going to be hard for Myrtle."

"It will be. But don't feel too bad for her. Myrtle's getting something out of this." Leo's eyes brightened. "She has that round-trip ticket to New

Zealand. She'll finally get to see a kakapo in real life."

Katie gaped at him. "She gets to keep the plane ticket?"

"Yeah, it wasn't purchased illegally. In fact—" He grinned at me. "—I can't say I'm much more of a fan of Branson than I was before. He's still dismissing that there is a poaching ring. Claims that he bets Owen was the one responsible for what we'd been noticing in the park. Which is ridiculous—he was part of it, but for sure not all. However, I think I'm starting to convince Officer Green, so maybe she can influence him."

"Susan?" I couldn't believe my ears. "She actually gives you the time of day?"

He winced. "I know she's horrible to you and your family. But she's one of the few in the department who will listen to my concerns."

How strange. I wouldn't have predicted that.

"It sounded like you were getting ready to say something good about Branson, though. What'd he do?"

Leo looked at Katie in confusion, and then his expression cleared. "Oh, right. I forgot. We were talking about Myrtle. I brought up Silas's plane ticket to Branson. We're betting the way Silas feels about Myrtle, he'd be willing to make the calls and get Silas's plane ticket switched to her name. If it works, she'll have two trips to New Zealand."

What a strange turn of events. "Silas would do that for Myrtle. Maybe it was love."

Katie had taken a bite of her almond croissant, and crumbs flew as she nearly choked. "Sure, if you call complete obsession, killing people who insult you, and building a rainforests to lock you in *love*."

"Okay, you have a point. A very good point." I laughed at her expression but shook my head. "It's a sweet thought, but I'm willing to bet Myrtle will trade in those plane tickets and use the money for the birds here. She won't use this experience to go see her kakapo. It would ruin it for her."

"Yeah. I bet you're right." Leo's smile faltered. "Didn't think of that."

I patted his arm, but switched the topic. "You weren't the only one thinking about things last night. Myrtle told me that Owen was paying double the annual fee. Do you think he was doing that to avoid suspicion?"

"Partly, yeah, I do." Clearly Leo had thought about this as well. "But honestly, that's one more reason I think it's clear we've got a ring happening. One poacher isn't going to be making that amount of money, at least not enough to throw twenty thousand at a bird club annually. But, yes. It kept suspicion off him, mostly, and gave him bigger access to Myrtle's resources, which aren't small. The police have the books now, so I can't get my hands on them, but someday. I bet those files will show how much Owen was using the bird club for the very thing it stood against."

Another motion outside the window caught my eye. Paulie and his two corgis had joined Carl in the fight against the snow-covered sidewalk. Flotsam and Jetsam looked to be ecstatic at the snowfall, though they were ecstatic—insane rather—about everything, and had Paulie slipping and tripping between the slick concrete and their rapidly weaving leashes.

Leo popped the last bite of his ham-and-cheese croissant into his mouth just as Sammy brought my dirty chai. Katie scowled but didn't say anything. After he finished chewing, Leo stood. "Well, I need to get to the park. Thanks for breakfast. See you ladies later."

I smiled and gave him a little wave as Katie lifted what was left of her almond croissant in a salute. "See you later, Smokey Bear."

As Leo walked away, Watson let out a yelp and rushed toward him.

Leo turned around, laughing, and knelt to one knee as he lavished affection on Watson. "I'm sorry, buddy. I'm so sorry. Bad park ranger, bad. How could I forget my favorite little man?"

Sammy had gone home over an hour before, and Katie and I were closing the shop. She'd just turned off all the lights upstairs and paused by the counter as I was putting the finishing touches to the books. "Pretty good day, huh?"

"Yeah. Funny what happens when I'm here to do my actual job. Sold over twenty-five books today."

"Wow! Almost like a real bookstore." She winked.

"Kinda." I laughed. "Of course, every single one of them was either a mystery or a book about birds."

"Estes loves its gossip. Now, if the next murder corresponds to a book genre, we're set."

"Don't say such horrible things. We're not hoping for murder."

She cocked an eyebrow but didn't give any further commentary. "Want me to hang out till you're done?"

"No, thank you. You gotta be exhausted. I won't be much longer." I walked around the counter and gave her a hug. "See you tomorrow?"

"Better believe it." Katie broke the embrace and walked toward the front door, giving the sleeping Watson a little wave before she left.

Another ten minutes, and I'd finished with the books and straightened the shelves of the few books we'd sold. Twenty-five wasn't that bad, at least by comparison. With the upstairs lights off, the book-shop truly was exactly how I'd envisioned it. It was perfect. The homey smells of the bakery above had already permeated the lower floor, making it even better than I'd dreamed. With a yawn, Watson stretched, stood, then padded over to me.

I gave him a quick scratch behind the ears. "No need to get up. I think we should hang out for a little bit. We spent all this time making this place exactly how we wanted, let's enjoy it. This time, without feeling guilty about being annoyed when a customer comes in."

Watson followed me to the mystery room and curled up under the sofa as I lit the fireplace and turned off all the other lights except the Victorian lamp. I slid a mystery off of one of the shelves, one I'd been meaning to read for ages, and curled up on the sofa. I opened to the first page but paused before I dove in, taking a second to enjoy the crackling fire, the soft glow created by the pale purple fabric, the comforting presence of my furry best friend nearby, and sighed.

Silas had attempted to make a haven for Myrtle. One that was everything she detested. I'd made my haven myself. Watson and me.

The fire popped again, and Watson let out a very undignified snort in his sleep.

My haven was perfect.

Katie's Ham & Gruyere Croissant recipe provided by:

2716 Welton St Denver, CO 80205

(720) 708-3026

Click the links for more Rolling Pin deliciousness:

RollingPinBakeshop.com

Rolling Pin Facebook Page

Katie's Ham & Gruyere Croissant Recipe

Ingredients:

    2 pounds and 8 ounces bread flour

    1 ounce salt

    4 ounces sugar

    1 pound and 12 ounces water

    1 ounce of yeast

    2.5 ounces butter

Butter to roll in – 1 pound and 10 ounces - softened and formed into 9" X 9" square. Place in refrigerator but don't let it get too firm. (This is separate from the 2.5 ounces of butter for the croissant mixture.)

Directions:

    1. Put yeast and water in bowl to activate yeast.

    2. After yeast is activated, place all other ingredients in bowl and with dough hook attachment, stir until combined. Continue kneading with dough hook for 10 minutes.

    3. Place dough in bowl and cover with plastic

wrap. Place in warm spot and let rise for about 30 minutes until doubled in size.

4. Punch down dough to deflate gases. Store in cold place until ready to use. Pull butter block from fridge and let get close to room temperature.

5. Roll the dough into a 14″ square with the middle being thicker than the edges.

6. Place square of soft butter on the dough and fold edges of dough over butter until completely covered. Put in refrigerator until both butter and dough are the same temperature.

7. Take dough from refrigerator and roll out to a rectangle shape. It should be three times as long as it is wide.

8. Fold the dough into three sections. Fold right side in first to cover the center third and then fold the left side to cover the folded right side.

9. Place dough in refrigerator for 2 hours. Remove and roll out to a rectangle size and fold over once in half.

10. Repeat steps 7-9.

11. Roll dough out to a large rectangle about 1/8th of an inch thick. Cut into two strips lengthwise.

12. Cut into even triangles with a pizza cutter or sharp knife.

13. Place piece of sliced ham and small amount of shredded Gruyere on each triangle. Starting with the wide end, begin rolling towards the point.

14. Place on parchment-lined baking sheet and place in a warm humid spot to let rise.

15. Brush with egg wash (2 eggs whisked with 1 Tbs water). Bake at 350 degrees until dark golden brown.

ABOUT THE AUTHOR

Reading the Cozy Corgi series is pretty much all you need to know about Mildred. In real life, she's obsessed with everything she writes about: Corgis, Books, Cozy Mountain Towns, and Baked Goods. She's not obsessed with murder, however. At least not at her own hands (nor paid for... no contract killing here). But since childhood, starting with Nancy Drew, trying to figure out who-dun-it has played a formative role in her personality. Having Fred and Watson stroll into her mind was a touch of kismet.

Website: Mildredabbott.com

AUTHOR NOTE

Dear Reader:

Thank you so much for reading *Bickering Birds*. If you enjoyed Fred and Watson's adventure, I would greatly appreciate a review on Amazon and Goodreads. Please drop me a note on Facebook or on my website (MildredAbbott.com) whenever you like. I'd love to hear from you.

I also wanted to mention the elephant in the room... or the over-sugared corgi, as it were. Watson's personality is based off of one of my own corgis, Alastair. He's the sweetest little guy in the world, and, like Watson, is a bit of a grump. Also, like Watson (and every other corgi to grace the world with their presence), he lives for food. In the Cozy Corgi series, I'm giving Alastair the life of his dreams through Watson. Just like I don't spend my weekends solving murders, neither does he spend his days snacking on scones and unending dog treats. But in the books? Well, we both get to live out our fantasies. If you are a corgi parent, you already know your little angel shouldn't truly have free reign of the pastry case, but you can read them spinets of Watson's life for a pleasant bedtime fantasy.

And don't miss book four, Savage Sourdough, coming February 2018. Keeping turning the page for sneak peek!

Much love, Mildred

PS: I'd also love it if you signed up for my newsletter. That way you'll never miss a new release. You won't hear from me more than once a month, nobody needs that many newsletters!

Newsletter link: Mildred Abbott Newsletter Signup

ACKNOWLEDGMENTS

A special thanks to Agatha Frost, who gave her blessing and her wisdom. If you haven't already, you simply MUST read Agatha's Peridale Cafe Cozy Mystery series. They are absolute perfection.

The biggest and most heartfelt gratitude to Katie Pizzolato, for her belief in my writing career and being the inspiration for the character of the same name in this series. Thanks to you, Katie, our beloved baker, has completely stolen both mine and Fred's heart!

Desi, I couldn't imagine an adventure without you by my side. A.J. Corza, you have given me the corgi covers of my dreams. A huge, huge thank you to all of the lovely souls who proofread the ARC versions of Cruel Candy and helped me look some-what literate (in completely random order): Ann

Attwood, Melissa Brus, Cinnamon, Kristell Harmse, Ron Perry, Rob Andresen-Tenace, Terri Grooms, Kelly Miller, TL Travis, Jill Wexler, Patrice, Lucy Campbell, Natalie Rivieccio, A.C. Mink, Rebecca Cartee, and Sue Paulsen. Thank you all, so very, very much!

A further and special thanks to some of my dear readers and friends who support my passion: Andrea Johnson, Fiona Wilson, Katie Pizzolato, Maggie Johnson, Marcia Gleason, Rob Andresen- Tenace, Robert Winter, Jason R., Victoria Smiser, Kristi Browning, and those of you who wanted to remain anonymous. You make a huge, huge difference in my life and in my ability to continue to write. I'm humbled and grateful beyond belief! So much love to you all!

SAVAGE SOURDOUGH PREVIEW

COMING FEBRUARY 2018

Opening the Cozy Corgi in Estes Park is a dream come true: small-town charm, fresh-baked bread, hours by the fire reading mysteries, and... murder.

For Winifred Page and her devoted corgi, Watson, the puzzle pieces of life are falling into place as they settle into their home in the Colorado mountains. Surrounded by family and friends, Fred begins to relax into the charm and beauty of being the owner of a bookshop and bakery.

The buzz of possible romance—though Fred wasn't looking for a relationship—has quieted as one of her suitors is no longer a viable option while the other has moved into the friend zone. But all thoughts of romance, wanted or not, fly out the window when Fred finds a dead body in the Cozy Corgi bakery... again.

Things get stickier when Fred's main suspect turns out to be a family member of one of the local police officers—the one who already despises Fred and her little dog. Determined not to let past grievances cloud her judgment, Fred tips her detective hat and pokes deeper into the murder investigation. But in a mystery that becomes smoke and mirrors, nothing is as it seems.

The revelations Fred unveil threaten not only her picture-perfect world but her very life....

A Cozy Corgi Mystery

Savage
Sourdough

MILDRED ABBOTT

CPSIA information can be obtained
at www.ICGtesting.com
Printed in the USA
BVHW080839171218
535784BV00001B/61/P